"Oh, my gosh." Sam took a breath, then pointed. "Look."

A tall black horse strutted apart from the herd. It was Moon. Sam was sure of it. She'd just recognized him when a movement farther up caught her eye.

"Is that the Phantom's son?" Brynna asked.

Sam nodded. "That's New Moon."

Through a piñon-choked pass, Sam saw a pale flicker. And there—dust floated in the wake of something moving fast. The Phantom raced toward the intruder.

Down by the turquoise river, the dun lead mare lunged with bared teeth. It was only a warning, and Moon knew it. Glittering like black satin, he slipped past and insulted her with a swivel of his heels.

"He's sure not trying to be sneaky about it," Brynna said. "Every horse down there can see he's trying to cut out that blood bay mare."

Hooves clattered on rock. Ace and Jeep shifted uneasily at the Phantom's warning neigh.

Sam turned toward Brynna, who looked at her with raised eyebrows.

"Stallions do a lot of pretending," Brynna said. "I've always heard they don't fight unless they must."

"I don't know," Sam said. "I think Moon's pushed his father too far."

Read all the books in the PHANTOM STALLION *series:*

Phantom Stallion

∞ 6 ∞
The Challenger

TERRI FARLEY

AVON BOOKS

An Imprint of HarperCollins*Publishers*

Library of Congress Catalog Card Number:
2002093142
ISBN 0-06-441090-0

First Avon edition, 2003

❖

Visit us on the World Wide Web!
www.harperchildrens.com

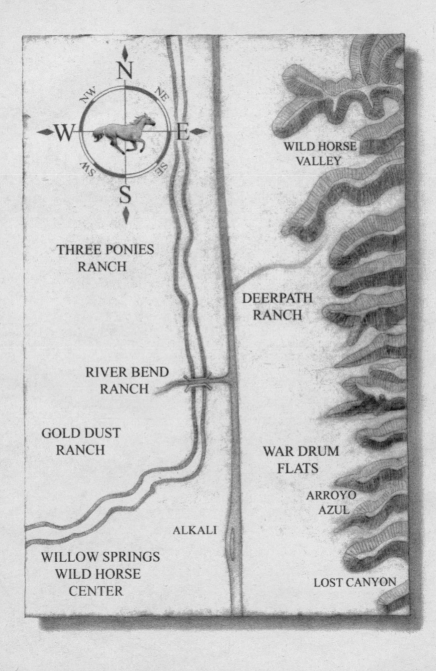

Chapter One

Samantha Forster had never felt so out of place.

Surrounded by the familiar scents of saddle soap, hay, and horses, she shouldn't have felt awkward, but she did. Sterling Stables was about as far as you could get from River Bend Ranch.

Not far in distance, Sam thought. She looked east. They were still in Nevada, just an hour from home. She could still smell sagebrush and hear the flutter of quail. She saw the Calico Mountains against the blue sky, too, but instead of white-peaked giants, they looked like miniature ice-cream cones.

Was the Phantom up in that rocky, windblown terrain? The thought of the mustang stallion with only his winter coat for protection made Sam shiver. The beautiful horses of Sterling Stables were sissies compared to the Phantom and his herd.

Shining like glass, a dozen Morgan yearlings grazed on acres of cross-fenced pastures. The irrigated grass rolled flat as green carpet around Sterling Stables' three long barns.

The stalls' half doors were open, showing the heads of dozens of perfectly groomed horses. About a block away from the barns, an arena held a variety of jumps built of candy-striped rails, hedges, and red brick. The arena was circled with a loamy oval marked by hoofprints.

"Could you pretend you're helping me pick a horse, instead of looking like a homesick pup?" Rachel Slocum muttered. Despite her irritation, the rich girl's faint smile stayed pasted in place. *How do you do that?* Sam wanted to ask, but Rachel's eyes warned her to focus.

"I *am* helping you," Sam said. "Or at least I would be, if you'd follow my suggestions."

Rachel closed her eyes, pretending to be patient. When she opened them, she considered the horse that was being paraded past for her approval.

"What do you think of this one?" Rachel asked.

A bay with a braided black mane trotted at the end of a short lead. His handler was a young woman wearing English jodhpurs, boots that shone with polish, and a white high-collared shirt just like Rachel's.

"He's beautiful." Sam shifted uncomfortably in her well-worn Western boots.

When Linc and Rachel Slocum picked her up at River Bend that morning, Sam had felt just right in her boots, jeans, and burgundy pullover.

The feeling hadn't lasted long.

At the first ranch, Rachel had window-shopped through a selection of Thoroughbred-cross endurance horses. Sam had loved watching the athletic animals, but her fun had faded when Rachel pointed out that Sam was dressed all wrong.

Who cares? Sam had wanted to ask, but she didn't. And even though she couldn't believe Rachel decided to leave without trying one of the endurance horses, Sam was relieved to drive away.

But this place was even worse.

At Sterling Stables, known for its select Morgan performance horses, Sam felt like a country bumpkin.

"Even I can see he's beautiful," Rachel said as the gelding trotted past again. "But should I buy him?"

"You haven't even asked how much they want for him," Sam said, keeping her voice low. Rachel's father, Linc, stood just a few feet away, talking on his cell phone.

Rachel smiled. "You know that doesn't really matter. I just want to know if *you'd* buy him. Will my brother think he's a great horse?"

"He looks healthy and strong. At halter, his gaits are smooth." Sam held her hand palm up, inviting Rachel to look around. "The stable certainly seems reputable, but you have to get on and ride, Rachel."

Rachel's eyes glittered with stubbornness as she pushed back a wing of dark hair. "Not in front of everyone."

Sam sighed. In spite of equestrian training in England and brush-up lessons here in Nevada, Rachel still wasn't a confident rider.

And Sam understood how she felt. A few months ago, after an injury and two years away from the ranch, she'd been nervous about riding again. But Sam didn't understand Rachel's willingness to take home an untried horse. What if it bucked? Or bit?

"I'm waiting for your opinion, Samantha." Rachel kept smiling, but she tapped her toe with impatience.

Sam decided she probably deserved this. She hadn't really come to help Rachel. She'd come to look at the horses.

If Rachel could hide her true feelings, why couldn't Sam? Maybe she needed more practice.

"Okay," she said, trying to sound pleasant. "Since you've given up the rodeo queen idea, and you have nothing in mind except buying a horse to impress your brother, just pick one you like."

Sam had kept her voice just above a whisper, unsure of whether Linc Slocum knew his daughter's plan, but she hadn't been quiet enough.

Linc Slocum snapped his cell phone shut.

"Honey, Samantha's right," he said. "That gal out there is Katie Sterling. She helps her dad run the place, and she wouldn't mind getting a horse ready for you to ride." Linc waited a second. Then, just in case Rachel hadn't taken the hint, he added, "You should probably ride the horse before we buy it."

"Daddy." Rachel's eyes were cold as she talked to

her father. "Did you bring your checkbook?"

In answer, Linc Slocum patted his pocket.

"Then that's all you need to worry about," Rachel said.

Before Sam absorbed the shock from Rachel's rudeness, the girl pointed at another stall.

"Wait. How about her?"

To Sam's surprise, Rachel walked toward a stall as if drawn by magnetism. "Mocha," said the brass plate on the stall door. The mare's head went up, and November sunshine shone on the neck she arched over her stall's half door.

Mocha's coat was the darkest possible brown, like fresh coffee. Her ears and eyes tracked Rachel's movements as she came closer.

Sam couldn't help turning to Linc Slocum. He grinned, and Sam thought they must be thinking the same thing: sometimes people and animals just click.

Katie Sterling noticed, too. She quit jogging the bay and led him back toward the stalls.

"I take it you're not interested in Glow-Boy." She sounded breathless as she patted the gelding's neck.

"No," Rachel said in a dreamy tone. "Just tell me about—Mocha."

"She's five years old, goes both English and Western, and she's really smart. Why don't I tack her up and you can see if you suit each other?"

Rachel shook her head. Her eyes refocused, this time on Katie Sterling. "What do you mean, smart?"

Perfect. Rachel believed horses were stupid, but

did she have to admit it? Sam didn't hold her head and moan, but Katie Sterling looked her way.

"Let's see." Katie sounded confused but willing to explain. "Someone mentioned cat tracks up your way, for instance. If you were ever to come near that cat, I think Mocha would stay calm and follow directions."

The young woman moved close enough that Glow-Boy and Mocha touched noses.

"Cat tracks?" Sam asked. "You mean like a bobcat?"

Linc Slocum leaned forward, listening for Katie Sterling's answer.

"I'm pretty sure it was a mountain lion," she said. "You know, a cougar."

"Up our way? Where?" Slocum demanded.

At his shout, Glow-Boy flinched. With a snort, the mare backed away from her stall door, and Rachel glared at her father.

"Maybe along a ridge?" Katie squinted as if trying to remember. "I couldn't say for sure, Mr. Slocum, but I bet it's nothing to worry about. Cougars are shy. About all you ever see of cats is their tracks."

"I'm not worried," Slocum insisted, but his face flushed red. "Who's saying this, now?"

"Let me think. It might have been Sheriff Ballard. He rides one of our horses in a mounted posse parade unit."

"Ya know his number?" Slocum opened his cell phone again.

"I don't, and I'm not certain it was him. With so

many horses, we get a lot of people through here. It might have been one of our boarders, or the vet —"

"Which one? The big guy or the scrawny blond fella with glasses?"

"I wish I could remember." Katie's voice was calm. Sam would bet she used the same tone to soothe nervous horses. "The Department of Wildlife could tell you more."

"They issue hunting licenses, too?"

Katie Sterling shrugged, then excused herself to put Glow-Boy back in his stall. While she was away, Linc Slocum paced.

Sam didn't much like the idea of a cougar prowling the ridge behind River Bend. She liked the idea of Linc Slocum with a rifle even less.

"So, what do you say?" Katie Sterling was striding back, arms loaded with a saddle and blanket, a bridle slung over one shoulder. "Ready to try Mocha?"

"Not today," Rachel said. "I have a few more horses to see, but I've no doubt we'll return."

Rachel rushed toward the Cadillac and Linc followed her, leaving Sam behind to face a surprised Katie Sterling.

"Thanks for your help," Sam said.

"My dad would tell me to shake your hand, but . . ." Katie lifted the saddle pointedly.

Sam smiled and said, "I bet Rachel will be back."

"Does she—please don't take this the wrong way—but does she even like horses?"

Katie's question made Sam feel included and accepted, even in her cowboy boots. She thought carefully before answering.

"Rachel likes to be in control," she said finally.

Katie grinned. "So does Mocha. Wouldn't *that* combination be fun to watch?"

Linc's Cadillac roared to life. A startled barn cat ran zigzag across the paddock as Sam waved good-bye to Katie. Sam hurried to the car and slipped into the backseat, still wondering what had attracted Rachel to Mocha.

"Where to?" Linc sounded distracted.

"To see that horse at Mrs. Ely's house, I guess." Rachel matched her hands palm to palm, but she wasn't praying. She tapped her fingernails, admiring her manicure.

Linc Slocum sighed. First thing this morning, he'd suggested they see Royal, a Quarter horse the Elys had gotten in trade for a tractor engine.

Rachel slid a CD into the car's player. Sam grimaced. She didn't share Rachel's taste in music, but she tried not to listen.

No one spoke as they sped down the highway.

Sam watched the Calico Mountains grow bigger on the horizon. She hoped the Phantom was tucked away safe with his herd. The last time she'd been in the valley of wild horses, the Phantom had been gone and his night-black son had acted as if he was in charge.

Known as New Moon, the black was almost as

handsome as his father. Son or not, though, the Phantom wouldn't allow Moon near his mares. Would he? She sighed. There was no way of knowing, unless she rode into the mountains to see for herself.

For months, the Phantom had trusted their friendship. He'd remembered her as the girl who'd raised him, but now the silver mustang was wilder than ever before. He'd been captured and forced to buck in a rodeo. After he'd come home, things had changed.

She had only one grain of hope. A few weeks ago, she'd found the stallion protecting a blind foal at the hot springs near Deerpath Ranch. He hadn't fled when she approached.

Maybe he'd come back to her after all.

As they passed the turnoff to Gold Dust Ranch, Linc Slocum kept his eyes on the ridge that soared above it. Watching for the cougar, no doubt. He was still watching as they passed the road to River Bend.

They'd almost reached the Elys' Three Ponies Ranch when Rachel began whining.

"Why does Mocha have to be a *smart* horse? That means she'll pull tricks if I don't pay attention every single minute, and I really want her."

Sam couldn't contain her curiosity any longer. "Why? What made you like her so much?"

Rachel half turned to look at Sam, in the backseat. "Even you must have noticed. Her coat *exactly* matches my hair."

Chapter Two

Three Ponies Ranch seemed deserted.

At first, Sam saw only a big gray gander. The bird announced the Cadillac's approach with a honk.

Then, as they drew closer, Sam saw Maxine Ely wave. It looked like Jake's mom was alone. She stood small and blond next to a corral.

Sam was the first one out of the car. She looked toward the barn, past it to the house, and wasn't surprised the Ely men were out of sight. Linc Slocum was not their favorite neighbor.

At the sound of hooves, Sam peered through the corral bars. Inside, Jake was mounting a big Quarter horse.

The minute Sam saw Royal, she knew two things: Jake had made a great deal, swapping a tractor engine for the fox-red stock horse; and Rachel wouldn't want him. Muscular and high-spirited, Royal would require an expert rider.

She kept her eyes on Rachel just the same. If she'd consider spending thousands of dollars on a horse because it matched her hair, there was no telling what else she'd do.

Linc Slocum stayed behind, frowning and pacing beside his car, while Sam and Rachel approached Mrs. Ely.

Linc shook his head and mumbled, but Sam was pretty sure he was talking to himself. She didn't think it was about Rachel's horse shopping, either.

Jake rode Royal in tight circles around the corral, then wheeled him on his heels and sent him galloping straight for the fence. A slight shift in Jake's position brought the gelding to a sliding stop.

"Wow," Sam said to Mrs. Ely as dust floated around them.

Maxine Ely nodded proudly as Jake touched the gelding into a swinging lope, and for a minute she seemed more like Jake's mom than Sam's history teacher.

Hatless and easy in the saddle, Jake rode with a natural grace even Rachel couldn't overlook. Though Rachel cared nothing about the horse, that didn't keep her from flirting with the rider.

"I'd have to be a lot stronger than I am to control him," Rachel said, pressing against the fence. When that didn't catch Jake's attention, she added, "Not everyone has muscular arms like you."

Involuntarily, Sam glanced at Jake's arms. He

hadn't buttoned his cuffs, so his sleeves blew back, baring his wrists and forearms. Big deal.

Muscles. A guy wouldn't really fall for that nonsense, would he? Jake was too smart to give Rachel a thrill by responding. But when a faint smile lifted one corner of his mouth, Sam wanted to scream.

Just then, she glimpsed Jake's brother Nate lurking inside the barn. Nate was a senior. Sam knew he'd get a kick out of seeing Rachel flirt with Jake, but even that wasn't enough to make Nate come out where he'd have to talk to Linc.

Mrs. Ely edged closer to Sam. "They don't look like a match to me."

"Who?" Sam yelped.

"Rachel and Royal, of course." Mrs. Ely tilted her head, watching Sam. "I don't think she'll buy him."

"Oh. No. I bet you're right." Sam felt herself blush and hoped Mrs. Ely would think her cheeks were red from the cold wind.

"The deal was, Luke let him make the swap, but Jake pays back the price of the tractor engine whether or not he sells Royal."

"He'll do it," Sam said. Jake was a fanatic about saving for college and a car.

Jake dismounted. Anyone could tell he didn't want to hang around and talk, but his mom didn't give him a choice.

"This is your deal, Jake," Mrs. Ely said. "I've got things to do up at the house."

"Mom." Jake's voice was level, but Sam saw his eyes dart toward Linc Slocum.

Mrs. Ely seemed not to notice. As she strolled toward the house, Jake looked after her, then glanced at Sam for help.

Yeah, right, Sam thought. After that smug little smile he'd given Rachel, the muscle man was on his own.

Jake's chest rose and fell in a silent sigh and he moved a few steps closer. As he did, Sam saw his jaw clench tighter. She'd bet the leg he'd broken last month still hurt.

"I'm afraid Royal might be too much for me." Rachel's tone invited Jake to contradict her.

He took his Stetson from a fence post and pulled it on before he answered. "Probably," he said.

Sam swallowed a laugh. It was a good thing Jake was interested in ranching and police work. He'd make a terrible salesman.

"That's done, then." Slocum stepped nearer.

"Daddy—" Rachel whined, but this time her father didn't listen.

"What do you know about a mountain lion up on the ridge?" Slocum asked Jake.

Something in his tone worried Sam, but Jake just shrugged.

"You've seen tracks, haven't you?" Slocum demanded.

Jake was well-known as a tracker. If there had been a mountain lion nearby Jake would have seen signs. But Jake stood even stiller than before.

Slocum took Jake's silence as a dare.

"C'mon, what's it to you?" Slocum taunted. "If there's a cat prowling behind my house, and yours, and the Forsters', we need to take care of it."

The more Slocum pushed, the more stubborn Jake became. His jaw set harder with each word Slocum said.

All at once, Sam thought of Buddy. Her pet calf was six months old. Would a mountain lion see her as easier prey than a deer?

"A cougar's tracks don't look much different from a big dog's," Jake offered, but Sam noticed he didn't answer Slocum's question.

Slocum noticed, too. "You could tell the difference."

"Maybe Jake has better things to do than snoop around the ridge," Rachel said, shifting so that her body angled toward Jake. "Besides, Dad, Katie Sterling said they were shy."

Jake watched Linc, then Rachel. His eyes barely moved, but Rachel didn't need much encouragement to start flirting all over again.

"Not that the idea of a dangerous animal being up there doesn't give me chills." Rachel skimmed her palms over the sleeves of her spotless white shirt. "But if Jake isn't worried about it, neither am I."

Linc crossed his arms and fixed Jake with a stare.

Finally, Jake spoke, but each word mocked Slocum's concern.

"The tracks are from a mother lion teaching her cub to hunt. The cub's a yearling or a little older. They're stalking squirrels and rabbits. Nothing big."

"I knew it!" Linc shook his index finger at Jake. "Doesn't mean they won't graduate to something larger, does it? And what if a rider was afoot?"

All at once, Sam understood Slocum's worry. He fell off his horse, Champ, pretty often. Just a few weeks ago, she'd caught the palomino and led him back to Linc, who'd been tottering across the desert in high-heeled cowboy boots.

Even before that, Slocum had hinted he was afraid of the big cats. When an escaped stallion called Hammer had tried to steal a mare from the Gold Dust Ranch, Linc had looked at the teeth rakings on her rump and asked Gram if they were from a cougar.

"If that happened," Slocum went on, "a person on the ground might make a pretty tempting tidbit, don't you think?"

"I think it's a pretty big switch, goin' from rabbits to riders. And cougars are solitary animals. It's not like they run in packs," Jake said.

"That's fine. I'm only getting a permit for one." Slocum threw the words down like a dare.

Jake's face grew darker, and Sam's mind raced, trying to think of something, *anything*, to say. Her instincts told her this could explode into a fight. If it did, Jake wouldn't lose, but he'd suffer for it. A teenager couldn't slug it out with an adult—no matter how much he deserved it—and not get in trouble.

She glanced at Rachel for help, but she was already standing by the Cadillac. Once the conversation had turned away from her, she'd lost interest.

On her own, Sam blurted, "Isn't there a certain season for hunting mountain lions? Like there is for other animals?"

"Ask him." Slocum's finger pointed at Jake again.

Jake shrugged. If he knew, he wasn't telling.

Linc passed his car keys from one hand to the other, making them jingle. "Time to go," he said, and turned back toward the car.

"Sam?" Rachel held the car door open, but Sam didn't get in.

"Thanks," she said. "It was fun, but I need to talk with Mrs. Ely about a history question. I'll, uh, have Jake drive me home later."

Jake didn't contradict her, thank goodness.

"On a Saturday?" Rachel raised an eyebrow, not believing Sam for a minute. "What kind of question could be so important?"

Sam figured it was just bad luck that Rachel was in her class. It didn't matter that Rachel was a junior repeating a freshman class. She still knew they had no homework.

"That's some serious kissing up." Rachel climbed into the car and slammed the door.

Before he joined her inside the Cadillac, Linc

stared at Jake across the vehicle's gleaming roof.

"Ely," he said.

Jake didn't answer, but he lifted his chin, showing Slocum he'd heard.

"When I go after that cat, don't get in my way."

A minute later, Linc gunned the engine so loudly, the Elys' goose honked a protest. Linc accelerated, sand and gravel spitting from the car's back tires. In seconds, nothing was left but dust rolling in interlocking swirls, chasing their own tails.

When Sam looked back over her shoulder, Jake was gone. He was walking toward the barn, leaving Royal tied at the corral. So Sam did what Jake always accused her of. She tagged along.

She didn't say a word. She got more out of Jake if she waited for him to talk.

Nate was more direct with his little brother.

"What was that all about?" he asked, keeping his eyes on the fresh straw he was forking into a stall. Just as Sam didn't try prying an answer out of Jake, Nate didn't even look at him.

"Old ways and new," Jake said.

That didn't make much sense, Sam thought. Neither did the way Jake watched his brother wield the pitchfork as if it were the most interesting thing in the world.

Sam sat down on a bale of straw, just out of the way, and kept listening.

"Is he part of the new way?" Nate jerked his head

in the direction Slocum had gone.

"Yeah." Jake leaned to pluck a piece of straw from the mound. "Make an enemy where there isn't one. Kill before there's a reason."

"Just in case." Nate put in.

Sam tried jumping to a conclusion. "You both think he's a coward," she guessed.

Nate gave a half smile. "Who'd say that about a neighbor?"

"You guys would, just not directly," Sam insisted.

"Look, the cougars aren't hurtin' anybody. The she-cat is limping." Jake sank down to sit next to her, then closed his eyes and rubbed his leg. When he opened them and saw Sam watching, he added, "They're not going after Buddy."

Startled, Sam said, "If you don't want me to make comments about that Indian mysticism stuff, you should stop reading my mind."

He pushed to his feet.

"Jake, I was teasing."

He walked out of the barn. Sam watched him go, feeling guilty, because she knew Jake hated any hint that he wasn't a hardheaded realist.

Sam jumped up and shouted after him. "I think Slocum's wrong! Does that make any difference?"

Jake didn't come back, and Nate didn't quit layering straw into a stall.

"He's putting Royal away, is all," Nate said.

"Right," Sam said. They both knew Jake was

mad. Through the barn door, she watched his jerky movements.

"How come," Sam said slowly, "whenever I'm around Jake, I end up picking sides?"

"Hmm," Nate said.

You're a lot of help, Sam thought. An almost-eighteen-year-old should be able to come up with something better than that.

"Maybe it's because Jake knows where he stands, and he won't back down." Nate looked pleased with himself—until he met Sam's eyes. "It's partly 'cause of you, he's so mad at Slocum."

"Because of me?" Sam squeaked. What could she have to do with Slocum and the cougars? "No way."

"He had this dream." Nate peered out the barn door to make sure Jake hadn't doubled back. "In it, something disturbed the cougars and they started killing wild horses—something like that."

"*Something* like that?" Sam demanded.

"It was just a dream," Nate said. "No big deal."

No big deal, Sam thought, except Jake had been so uneasy about the dream, he'd told Nate.

She swallowed hard. *No big deal*, except that he'd risked a fight to discourage Linc's interest in the cougar.

And, she decided, it was a very big deal when Jake was ignoring Royal to stare up at the ridge as if something terrible was coming their way.

Chapter Three

Sam didn't have a chance to nag Jake for details of his dream, and she had only a few moments of silence to worry over the wild horses.

Gram pulled into Three Ponies Ranch, looking rushed and bothered. She waved Sam into the Buick before she could say a proper good-bye to the Elys.

Sam knew they were going to meet Brynna for dinner at Clara's Diner, but why was Gram in such a hurry?

"You'll need time to shower and change," Gram explained as they pulled onto the highway.

"We're just going to Clara's, right?"

Gram nodded. "I want you to wear a dress." She lifted one hand from the steering wheel and rubbed at the line between her brows, as if telling herself to relax.

Gram was keeping something secret, but Sam didn't ask what. She had an outfit she'd been saving for an "occasion," and this might be the best chance she'd get.

"How about my black skirt and new sweater?"

"Fine." Gram sawed at the wheel, swerving off the road and over the River Bend bridge much too fast.

Instead of barking a greeting, Blaze scampered out of the way. He bounded onto the bunkhouse porch, tail wagging at half-mast.

A cloud of steam still hung in the bathroom when Sam went in. She heard Dad whistling in his bedroom, and froze.

The last time she'd heard Dad whistle . . .

Dad *never* whistled.

After showering and blow-drying her hair into a smooth cap, Sam pulled on her new scoop-necked sweater. Jen, Sam's best friend, had insisted Sam buy it the last time they'd been at Crane Crossing, the mall in Darton.

Sam tugged at the sweater's hem and considered it in the mirror. Not too tight or too baggy, the sweater fit fine. She was almost embarrassed that it matched the reddish brown of her hair. On the other hand, it was a sweater, not a horse.

Sam leaned close to the mirror to put on rose-tinted lip gloss. Why was Gram making such a big deal about this dinner?

"Ready to go, hon?" Dad leaned in the doorway.

His dark hair was wet and slicked back above the

collar of a blue-and-white checked shirt. His jeans were new, and he was being entirely too nice.

Sam knew she couldn't comment on that, but now she was even more worried.

"Something wrong?" Dad asked. His smile started to fade.

Don't be a brat, Sam told herself.

"Nothing's wrong, except I'm so hungry I'm hallucinating a mountain of Clara's fries floating in midair," Sam chattered. "And I'm in need of decent company after spending all day with the Slocums!"

Dad grinned instead of reprimanding her. He had an obsession with manners, so that was another bad sign.

Sam put down her brush, picked up her coat, and followed Dad. Gram looked up at them as they came downstairs. For a second, Gram's bottom lip trembled, then her hand covered her mouth. All at once, she rummaged in her purse as if she'd lost something.

"Are you okay, Gram?" Sam could have sworn Gram was about to cry.

Gram cleared her throat. "It's nice to see you with a touch of lipstick, is all."

"Good," Sam said. "Because I'm probably the first person in the entire history of Clara's who's ever worn makeup."

"Oh, now . . ." Gram began.

"Unless," Sam added, "maybe a rodeo clown stopped in before he'd scrubbed off his greasepaint."

For some reason, both Gram and Dad thought that was very funny. They were still laughing as they all piled into the car.

Sam wondered why neither of them guessed she was babbling out of absolute fear.

They parked the Buick and approached the diner.

"Order anything on the menu," Dad said as he reached for Clara's squeaky front door.

The dark feeling had faded on the drive over, but now it came back.

What if she was sick? Was there some aftereffect of her riding accident no one had mentioned to her that would kick in about now?

Wait. Sam reined in her imagination. Dad wouldn't smile if she was in trouble. Still, his generosity needed testing.

"Jumbo fried prawns?" Sam asked. "And chocolate upside-down cake?"

"Sure, why not?" Dad pushed open the diner door and a bell rang their arrival.

Sam's confusion vanished the minute she saw Brynna Olson sitting alone at a corner table.

Tonight, Brynna wore no uniform, no tight French braid, no look of cold professionalism. Her hair streamed red and ripply over the shoulders of a bright blue dress. Brynna's smile lit her whole face, and she bounced to her feet as if she couldn't stay seated another instant.

In one long stride, Dad was next to Brynna. His arm curved around her waist before he looked at Sam with raised eyebrows.

They were so obvious about what was coming next, Sam couldn't help laughing. "Yes?" she asked.

Gram pulled out a chair and sat. Sam did, too, though it was way too late to worry about attracting attention. Even Clara, with her waitress pad and food-smudged uniform, was watching them with a sappy smile.

Dad leaned across the table and flattened his hand on Sam's. "Tonight's a celebration, Sam. I've asked — well, Brynna and I have decided to get married."

Dozens of questions swirled in Sam's mind, but she wasn't shocked or sad.

"Congratulations," she said. Then, because that sounded too stiff, she added, "You guys look really happy."

"We are, Sam." As Brynna's hand came down on top of Dad's, Sam saw the silver ring set with a small round diamond. "I'll do my best to be the *un*wickedest stepmother who's ever lived." She took a deep breath. "I don't want to change your life, or take up too much of your dad's time, or anything like that."

Sam believed her, but when she pictured Brynna Olson living in her house, it felt weird. Then an even worse picture flashed through her imagination.

"We *are* all going to live at the ranch, right?" she asked.

"Of course," Dad said. "The only way I'm leaving River Bend is in a casket."

"Wyatt, don't be morbid," Gram scolded.

Morbid, maybe, but it made Sam feel better.

"When are you having the wedding?" Sam asked.

Clara overheard the question as she set out glasses of ice water. She didn't whoop with surprise, just acted as if she'd seen this coming long ago.

"Best wishes, you two. I'll be back to get your order in a minute." Clara smiled and tapped her pencil's eraser against her order pad. "Dessert's on the house."

While Brynna thanked Clara, Dad answered Sam's question.

"It'll be soon," he said. "Just after Christmas, I think. While you're on winter break."

That *was* soon. Thanksgiving was coming up. Sam imagined all the kitchen bustle that came with the holiday, and snatched a quick look at Gram.

She looked like she was holding her breath.

Sam's irritation that Gram had known about the engagement and kept quiet vanished. Even if Gram was happy, she must feel worried, too. Since Mom's death years ago, Gram had run the house and garden, ruled the ranch in partnership with Dad, and been the undisputed queen of the kitchen. How much would change?

Before dinner came, they toasted Dad and Brynna with soda. Sam had eaten only two of her jumbo shrimp when Brynna asked if she'd act as maid of honor.

Sam thought the maid of honor was the girl who walked down the aisle before the bride. She pictured herself moving toward the front of the church with everyone watching. That was a little scary.

"I'm not sure how to do it," she admitted. "I've never been a bridesmaid before."

"And I've never been a bride." Brynna laughed. "But Grace knows a lot." She nodded at Gram. "She's agreed to bake the wedding cake, and Mrs. Coley said she'd make our dresses. I'll get some books and we'll learn together. It'll be fun."

Sam agreed. It *would* be fun, but as Brynna chatted and planned with Gram, Sam already missed the other Brynna, the tough-minded professional who cared more about mustangs than satin and lace.

Sam had just taken a bite of chocolate upside-down cake when Brynna pushed her hair back and straightened her shoulders.

"Can't it wait?" Dad asked, as if he knew what Brynna was about to say.

"It could, but Sam won't mind." Brynna looked sure of herself.

Sam licked some frosting from her fork and glanced between the two of them. "Mind what?" she asked.

"Talking about the Phantom," Brynna said.

"What's wrong?"

"Probably nothing, but one of the choppers was flying over Lost Canyon and saw a herd. There were a few light-colored horses, and I wondered if you thought it was possible the Phantom was wintering in Lost Canyon."

"How would she know?" Gram asked.

"Sam's been gone the last two winters," Dad pointed out.

"Instinct, I guess." Brynna waited.

Sam stopped with her fork halfway to her mouth. She pictured Lost Canyon. It was a lot lower than the Phantom's hideaway in the Calico Mountains. From War Drum Flats, you went uphill, but then down into the canyon. Arroyo Azul, a gully holding a turquoise stream centered on the canyon's floor, was lower still.

A lower altitude meant less snow and a warmer place to winter.

She didn't know how far Lost Canyon stretched into the mountains. She only knew the canyon was old. Jake had told her stories about Indians who'd lived there with fast, loyal war ponies. And once, she'd followed a wild horse rustler in there.

She shivered at the memory of that close call and then stopped.

"I bet I know where they'd be, if they're in Lost Canyon at all," Sam said. "Do you know Arroyo Azul?"

Brynna shook her head.

"I could show you," Sam offered.

"And break your neck trying," Dad added.

"Dad, I won't ride down there." Sam caught her breath, remembering the sandstone shelves and the stream she'd only seen from above. "You can see it from the path."

"That sounds safe enough," Brynna said.

Dad made a disapproving sound.

"But I don't know how the horses get in there," Sam told Brynna.

"Keep it that way," Dad said. "And if you two are thinking of riding in that canyon tomorrow, watch out. Don't go till the ice is melted in the dog's water dish."

Sam smiled. Her family had always measured cold by the thickness of ice crust on the dog's bowl.

"And watch where you let the horses step," he added. "There's no telling what the storms have washed loose."

"Brynna knows how to spot avalanche danger," Gram said, but her words were a reminder.

"Are we going?" Sam asked Brynna.

"If you want to," she said. "I need to go anyway."

Something in the way Brynna said it worried Sam. "Why?"

"Only part of that canyon is Bureau of Land Management land," she explained. "If there is a herd in there, I hope it's on it."

"Who owns the rest of it?" Sam asked. An ugly thought floated into her mind. "Not Linc Slocum?"

"Not Linc," Brynna said. "Part of Lost Canyon belongs to the local tribes."

"Oh, my." Gram sipped from her water. "That could be a problem."

"Why?" Sam shifted in her seat, facing Gram. While Gram searched for words to explain, Sam turned toward Brynna and Dad.

"It's not likely they'd want to," Brynna said, "but they could trap the horses and keep them or sell them."

"What?" Sam screeched loud enough that Clara turned to see what was going on. "Wild horses are protected by the government. Everyone knows that. Catching them is against the law."

"Sorta," Dad said, tilting his hand back and forth.

"Sorta?" Sam asked.

"BLM has pretty cordial relationships with the tribes, but the Indians are a sovereign nation. It's like they have their own country within this country," Brynna explained. "So they don't exactly have to obey U.S. laws."

"Even the ones protecting wild horses?" Sam asked.

"That's about the size of it." Dad raised his hand. "Check, please," he said, and Clara nodded that she was on her way. "The tribes have their own laws, and there's nothing you or the BLM can do about it."

Brynna scooted closer to Dad and leaned her head against his shoulder. "What Wyatt said isn't precisely true," she said pleasantly. Then, looking at Sam, she lowered her voice to a whisper. "I'll explain tomorrow."

"Ain't nothing to explain," Dad shot back, just as pleasantly.

He and Brynna sat up straight, staring at each other as Clara approached their table.

"This is goin' to be a real interestin' marriage, Wyatt." Clara put the check facedown on their table. "Yep, if nothing else, you all will be fun to watch."

Chapter Four

Sunday morning, Sam went to church with Gram and Brynna.

"By the time we get back, the ice should be melted off Blaze's water dish—right, Dad?" Sam joked as she climbed into Gram's Buick, but Dad just waved them on their way.

They shared a pew with Mrs. Coley, and because they were early, the women made wedding plans until the organ's chords announced the first hymn.

Sam couldn't figure out why she suddenly felt disloyal.

Mom is dead. Sam made herself think the words in a hard, blunt way. That didn't help. Some childish part of her brain still believed she and Dad should keep waiting for Mom to return.

She needed to talk with Gram or Dad about her mother. She always felt better after she did. She'd bet, though, that Mom wouldn't want Dad to stay alone if he could be happy with someone else. True love wasn't selfish.

Sam quit singing because of the hard lump in her throat. The altar's harvest leaves and candles blurred before her eyes.

"Samantha?" Gram asked quietly as Sam quit singing.

Sam rubbed her eyes. "I might need glasses or something," she mumbled. "I can't see too well."

If Gram didn't buy that excuse, she didn't mention it.

Two hours later, Sam mounted Ace. He danced with impatience while Brynna finished saddling Jeepers-Creepers. A rangy, flea-bitten Appaloosa with a skinny rattail, Jeep wasn't the prettiest horse on River Bend Ranch, but he was a quick, dependable mount.

Ace swung his head around and peered up through his forelock at Sam.

"Ready to get going, pretty boy?" she asked.

The gelding tossed his black mane. The star on his forehead shone extra white in the cold, cloudless afternoon. He hurried Sam with a low nicker, then nudged the toe of her boot.

"In a minute," she told him, but Ace didn't want to wait. He watched the other horse and rider. The instant Brynna's jeans hit the saddle, Ace stepped out.

The cold boards of the bridge gave the horses'

hoofbeats a hollow sound as they left River Bend.

Sam wanted to let Ace run, but Brynna kept Jeep at a jog and she seemed determined to start a conversation.

"I wanted to ride Popcorn," Brynna said as they approached War Drum Flats. "But since you've had him under saddle for such a short time, I'm not sure it would be fair."

Sam nodded, feeling Ace bunch beneath her.

"Taking him where there might be a wild herd, I mean," Brynna added, in case Sam had missed her point.

"Yeah," Sam said, nodding. "You're right."

Judging by the way Brynna's lips pressed together, that wasn't a great response.

"Why don't we let them run here?" Sam suggested. "Ace is ready to stretch his legs."

"I haven't had a good run for a while, either," Brynna agreed.

For five minutes, the two horses ran together. Galloping into the frosty air, Sam wished she'd worn something heavier than her fleece jacket. Once they were in Lost Canyon, though, stone walls would block the wind, and she should warm up.

After they'd crossed War Drum Flats, Ace was willing to settle into a jog. When Jeep slowed to match Ace's gait, Sam glanced at Brynna.

Strands of red hair had blown loose from Brynna's braid and they straggled over her flushed cheeks. She looked happy. Sam knew she was lucky to be getting a stepmother who loved to ride.

Mountain mahogany flanked the path up to Lost Canyon. Its branches rattled, although Sam couldn't feel the breeze. She couldn't feel her fingers, either, curled tight around her reins. She really should have worn gloves, like Brynna.

As they started up the path to Lost Canyon, the two horses tried to walk abreast.

Brynna was an expert rider. She must have noticed there wasn't room for the two horses side by side, but she seemed more interested in talking.

"Have you been over to Mrs. Allen's place lately?" she asked.

Sam shook her head and reined Ace in behind Jeep.

"I hear she's calling her new venture the Blind Faith Mustang Sanctuary," Brynna said over her shoulder.

"Great," Sam answered.

She was being as uncommunicative as Jake, but she couldn't help it. Brynna was such an experienced rider, she could concentrate on something else while the horses worked out who ranked higher in this herd of two. Sam wasn't that good.

Just ahead, Jeep whisked his tail in irritation. Was he about to kick? Ace didn't want to lead, but Jeep didn't want to be followed.

Sam had just recognized the cracked rock on her left when Brynna stopped her mount. Two months before, water had dripped from the crevice in that rock and Dark Sunshine, snatched by Sam from the rustlers, had stopped there to drink.

Now Brynna had chosen this wide spot in the trail to look irritated.

"I don't know if you're trying to be difficult—"

"I'm not," Sam interrupted. "It's just that the horses are working things out and I need to pay attention. I'm still just a teeny bit afraid of getting bucked off."

Sam watched Brynna's lids lower over her blue eyes. She let her reins rest on Jeep's neck as she watched Sam, deciding whether to believe her.

"You know, don't you, that your dad and I love each other." Brynna said the words carefully. "That's why we're getting married."

"Well, that's what I figured," Sam said sarcastically. Why was Brynna talking to her as if she were a toddler?

Ace's hindquarters shifted nervously. Sam laid a hand on his neck. The move seemed to steady her, too. She took a deep breath, deciding to tell the full truth. "It's just that I keep thinking of my mom," Sam admitted.

Brynna sighed. "I don't blame you, but it's not our fault your mom is gone," Brynna said gently. "You might as well blame the herd of antelope your mother swerved to miss."

"I know," Sam said.

Both Gram and Dad had told her that her mother's last action was typical. Everyone had been saddened, but no one had been shocked to hear that Louise Forster had driven her car off the road rather than crash into a herd of wild antelope.

"I was hoping," Brynna said, slowly, "that you'd be glad your father's finally happy."

"He was happy with me and Gram!" Sam heard how bratty the words sounded as soon as she uttered them.

Brynna could have snapped right back, but she didn't. Instead, her voice softened. "Of course he was, but this is different."

In the quiet that followed, Jeep moved aside so that Ace could lick the damp rock. Sam let him.

Overhead, a hawk's cry rang, but when Sam looked up, the blue sky was empty.

"Wyatt has told me things about your mom that made me think we could have been friends." Brynna held her reins in one hand and took off her deerskin gloves by nipping at the leather covering her index fingers, then tugging the gloves off.

"Like what kinds of things?" Sam asked.

"Probably stuff you know." Brynna looked a little embarrassed. Now that she had both gloves off, she flexed her fingers.

"Tell me anyway," Sam encouraged her.

"Did you know she worked with a mechanic in Darton to rebuild the engine on her VW bug when she found out she was pregnant?"

Sam shook her head. "That's kind of weird."

"Wyatt said she not only wanted it new and reliable, she wanted to know how the engine was put together so that if anything went wrong without Wyatt there to help, the two of you wouldn't be stranded and helpless."

Sam thought of a snapshot in the family picture album. In it, her mom wore overalls and long auburn pigtails. She could imagine Mom tying a bandanna over her hair, then sliding under a car with a wrench.

"Thanks. No one ever told me about that." Sam pulled Ace away from the rock and backed him up a few steps. "We can keep going if you want."

"In a minute." Brynna drew a deep breath. "Sam, I love your dad and I want us to be a happy family, but I know I can't replace your mom. After all, she gave him you."

Sam didn't know what to say, and Brynna saved her the trouble of thinking of something.

"Let's go find some wild horses," she said, "so I don't have to listen to the I-told-you-so's from everyone who said this was a job better done from a helicopter." Brynna put Jeep into a quick walk up the trail and Sam followed.

How deep was Lost Canyon? Sam had only ridden in a few miles, but she'd seen the Phantom there and imagined some back entrance to the canyon from the Calico Mountains.

Sam watched Ace's ears. The gelding was alert, but he wasn't showing the excitement he usually did when they were near other mustangs.

The canyon walls narrowed, putting them in shadow as they rode on. They passed a cottonwood tree that had managed to survive with its roots sunk in the cleft of a rock. Down at River Bend, cottonwoods and aspens still showed leaves of gold. Here, the altitude and weather had stripped the cottonwood of leaves. Its gray branches were cracked and bare.

Sam pulled her jacket closer. The lack of sun and the wail of wind around the rocks made her shiver.

As they approached the overlook to Arroyo Azul, Sam realized she was actually leading Brynna to a place where she might find the Phantom.

Sam wouldn't think of showing anyone the stallion's haven in the Calico Mountains. Not Jake, Dad, or even Jen, but Arroyo Azul wasn't a secret. Brynna already knew where to search. With Sam's help, Brynna would find him sooner, without the swooping racket of helicopters.

Besides, Brynna was trying to protect the mustangs, not catch them, and that made all the difference.

"Remember the young black horse you mentioned? The Phantom's son, you thought, who took over the herd while Karla Starr had the Phantom?" Brynna glanced over her shoulder to see Sam nod. "I wonder if he's still with the herd?"

"I don't know," Sam mused. "The Phantom must have driven him out once, because he was with a bachelor band. But then he was back with the herd when the Phantom was gone."

"Horses try to stay with their family herd," Brynna said. "I wonder if he was in charge or just hanging around because his father wasn't there to drive him out?" Brynna said.

"He *thought* he was in charge." Sam recalled how the young horse had pranced and threatened. "But the lead mare didn't seem convinced he was the boss."

All at once, the trail widened. Sun struck them and Ace seemed to trot on tiptoe.

"We're getting close," Sam said, and then they stopped. Even the saddle horses stared at the vista that suddenly appeared on their left.

Sandstone cliffs were stacked like rows of seats in an amphitheater, and a turquoise stream marked the bottom of Arroyo Azul. Horses moved like wind-up toys, dwarfed by the distance between the trail where Brynna and Sam sat their horses and the bottom of the arroyo.

Ace gave a short snort and Jeep echoed it. Both geldings grew tense as they listened for sounds from the horses down below.

"We have to go down closer to watch," Sam said.

"Why? They're here, and I've got a good enough idea of where they are that I can check our maps and see if they're on BLM or BIA land."

"There's got to be a path down," Sam said, "and we've got to take it. Look."

Sam pointed as Ace and Jeep whinnied.

Silver against the pink-gold sandstone, the stallion stood silent, but he saw them. Sam's heart swelled with excitement.

Though he stood a half mile away, across thin air, the Phantom flipped his heavy mane and tossed his head in greeting. He saw all of them, but he was welcoming her.

She wanted to call back to him, using his secret name, but she didn't. She wanted to fly across the canyon, circle his neck with her arms, and hug him, but she couldn't. Not even if she were standing beside him.

Sam ached with what she'd lost.

Before he'd been betrayed by humans, the stallion had let Sam stroke his sleek hide and bury her face in his mane. Before, she'd finger-combed that thick mane and braided a bracelet of loose silvery hairs. When she gave that bracelet away to a girl who needed its magic, Sam hadn't guessed the Phantom might never trust her to get that near him again.

"We've got to move closer," she repeated, "just to watch."

With silent skill, Brynna turned Jeep toward a deer trail. To human eyes, it was faint, as if a bit of dull green had been erased from the hillside, but the horses followed its twisting path downward.

Trusting Ace to keep his feet, Sam turned in her saddle, still watching the Phantom.

In her imagination, she could lure him to the river again. She could lay hands on his warm back. Her touch would tell him she'd never hurt him. He'd understand she could ride him and then slip from his back and set him free.

Across the canyon, the Phantom rose in a half rear. Sam tried to believe he wanted their friendship as much as she did.

A crunch and shower sounded as Jeep's hoof struck a piece of loose sandstone and crushed it. Taking no chances, Ace rocked back, then vaulted forward, leaping over the spot.

Hazards were all around. This was no place for daydreaming.

"Doing okay?" Brynna called back.

"Sure. Ace is more surefooted than—"

Scattered neighs and a tumult of hooves interrupted. Something was going on. Whatever had disturbed the mustangs was hidden by a dust cloud swirling over them.

Sam glanced up. They were pretty close to the herd, about two city blocks away, but she could no longer see the Phantom. No silver shadow glittered against the pink sandstone. He'd gone to protect his family.

"Oh, my gosh." Sam took a breath, then pointed. "Look."

A tall black horse strutted apart from the herd. It was Moon. Sam was sure of it. She'd just recognized him when a movement farther up caught her eye.

Through a piñon-choked pass, Sam saw a pale flicker. And there—dust floated in the wake of something moving fast. The stallion raced toward the intruder.

"Is that his son?" Brynna asked.

Sam nodded. "That's New Moon."

Down by the turquoise river, the dun lead mare lunged with bared teeth. It was only a warning, and Moon knew it. Glittering like black satin, he slipped past and insulted her with a swivel of his heels.

Moon didn't pause to see her reaction. He shoved into the herd of mustangs, scattering bays and sorrels, mares and foals. The tiniest of the lot, a roan filly whose red coat looked like it had been covered with a sifting of sugar, raced to get out of Moon's way.

"He's sure not trying to be sneaky about it," Brynna said. "Every horse down there can see he's trying to cut out that blood bay mare."

Hooves clattered on rock. Ace and Jeep shifted uneasily at the Phantom's warning neigh.

Sam turned toward Brynna, who looked at her with raised eyebrows.

"Stallions do a lot of pretending," Brynna said. "I've always heard they don't fight unless they must."

"I don't know," Sam said. "I think Moon's pushed his father too far."

Chapter Five

*A*s if Moon heard Sam's worry, he let the blood bay return to the other mares. He whirled to face his sire.

Sam and Brynna rode a little closer, drawing rein at a relatively flat spot where bare aspen stood tall and white. Here, Jeep and Ace could stand together, and they could all watch.

Sam felt a little sick. If she were observing this on television, she wouldn't hear hooves pounding bone and teeth tearing skin. Or if she did, it would all be pretend.

The Phantom stopped about ten feet from his son and laid his ears back. Any horse could read the stallion's irritation, but Moon didn't move away.

The Phantom stamped a front hoof. He looked impatient, but Moon switched his tail as if he didn't care.

He's asking for it, Sam thought.

Still, the stallion didn't treat Moon like a challenger. Lowering his silvery head, the Phantom bared his teeth and snaked his neck in the scolding, herding move he'd use on any mare or foal that disobeyed.

For a second, Moon hesitated. His head turned slightly. His lips moved, as if chewing over the problem of his father's strength. His tail drooped and he glanced at the mares.

All at once, wind raced through the canyon. Its scent carried reminders of the days Moon had ruled these mares.

Inky torrents of mane flew around Moon's head and neck. He bobbed his head, higher every time, refusing to be scolded. Neck arched, tail flung high, he defied his father by refusing to retreat.

Moon didn't know what he was getting into. Even though he stood taller than his sire, the Phantom had the broad chest and thick muscles of a mature stallion.

"This is all play-acting," Brynna reassured Sam. "Stallions don't want to draw blood. Even if he's a sure winner—like the Phantom—he could be hurt. He knows even a small injury might make him slower. And that would be bad for the herd."

"You didn't see him fight Hammer," Sam said. "When Hammer didn't back down, the Phantom was all over him."

Sam would never forget the loud and brutal fight.

Both stallions had been streaked with blood.

The Phantom gave Moon time to size him up while Sam and Brynna watched in silence.

The horses stood still for so long, Sam noticed the shiny rocks around them. They must have worn a skim of ice earlier, but now it had melted off. The smell of wet earth wasn't flowery like it was in spring. Autumn was ending and winter was nearly here.

Sam took turns holding her reins with one hand while she tucked the other under the warmth of her jacket.

Time's up. With a jerk of his head, the Phantom signaled his son to fight or flee.

The silver stallion approached like a king. Moon fidgeted, but he held his ground until the Phantom stood in front of him. The horses stood eye-to-eye, then the Phantom moved forward, giving his son's forehead a shove.

Moon retreated a step and the Phantom came after him, jostling his head again.

All at once, Moon reacted like a teenager who'd been pushed too far. With a high-pitched squeal, the black rose up on his hind legs. The silver stallion must have known what would happen, because he reared at exactly the same instant.

For a moment, they stood like mirrored reflections, one dark and one light.

The Phantom dodged past the black's threshing forelegs, ducking to grab his mane. He tugged, pulling the black off balance, then dodging out of the way.

Moon fell, but he bolted up at once. Looking anxious, he trotted a circle around his father, but Sam could see he'd skinned his knees.

"He sparred with Yellowtail and Spike and he always won," Sam said.

"Who?"

"A bay and a chestnut in his bachelor band. Mrs. Coley named them. We saw them play-fighting once, and Moon was clearly the best. I think he's confused because the Phantom's not such an easy opponent."

"Look at the mares," Brynna said.

The Phantom's herd grazed, unconcerned. When Moon gave a series of short snorts, the mares looked up, but they knew the outcome of the fight. They were indifferent about how the Phantom won.

All but the blood bay. The mare Moon had tried to steal seemed interested. Searching for a better view, she stepped away from the herd.

Sudden hoofbeats made Sam look back to the stallions.

"He's giving it another try," Sam said.

Suddenly, Moon darted toward the Phantom. Ears pinned, head flat, he grabbed for the gray. The Phantom swerved, but the smear of foam on his neck showed how close Moon had come to biting him.

"Too close," Brynna said. "Now the Phantom's getting mad."

Sam heard Brynna swallow, and there was

something about her nervousness that made Sam glad. They both knew battles like this had been acted out for centuries, but neither could accept this one as no big deal.

The fight turned loud as the stallions changed tactics. Hooves skittered, then hammered on hide as they launched powerful kicks with their hind legs. Guttural neighs were wrenched from both horses.

The blood bay mare trotted closer, but she didn't get far. The lead mare drove her back with the others.

Distracted by the skirmish between the lead mare and the blood bay, Moon's head swung away from the Phantom.

The silver stallion charged.

Surprised, Moon broke into a reluctant run. From above, it looked to Sam like there was only one way out of the canyon. Scored with red scratches and gouges, Moon galloped toward it.

When the tiger dun lead mare joined in the pursuit, the Phantom stopped, letting her take over.

As he returned to his herd, the little roan filly raced out to greet him. The Phantom shook his head, and she sprinted back to her mother.

The stallion trotted around his herd, circling again and again.

"He's counting to make sure they're all there," Brynna joked, but her words were breathy, as if she was unsettled by what might have happened.

A low, angry squeal made Sam look toward

Moon. "It's not over." She gasped.

Moon refused to be driven out by the dun mare. He wheeled at a run and came charging back.

"Why doesn't he just quit?" Sam demanded.

"He's braver than he is smart," Brynna said.

Around them, the wind picked up again. The aspens' bare white branches clacked together like bones.

The Phantom must have expected Moon's stubbornness, because he ran toward him at full speed. Sam drew a shaky breath.

The Phantom was terrifying and beautiful. His dished head, large eyes, and wind-drinking nostrils had always shown his Arabian ancestry, but now he looked primitive, like a throwback to some fierce desert warhorse.

Sam could imagine him galloping over searing sands, facing flapping white robes and knife-edged swords. She longed for a camera. One flick of the shutter could capture his ivory power. She'd call the photo "Rage."

The Phantom rammed into Moon's shoulder. Thousands of pounds of muscle and bone collided, and both horses staggered.

"If he goes down, it's all over, isn't it." Brynna's words weren't really a question.

Sam knew Brynna was right. If Moon fell and the Phantom attacked, the younger stallion could be killed.

Instead, he staggered toward the mouth of the canyon, burst into a clumsy run, then hit his stride. Like spokes on a black wheel, Moon's legs moved in a smooth pattern as they carried him away from his family. Then he disappeared.

The Phantom didn't celebrate. He strode back to his herd, shaking his mane and uttering small nickers to the mares.

"'All in a day's work, ladies,'" Brynna said, pretending to speak for him.

Sam laughed. Brynna's humor helped wipe away the melancholy of seeing the young horse lose. Of course, he had to, and given a choice, Sam would have wanted him to. The Phantom was the best protector for this herd, and he would always be her favorite.

Still, she felt sorry for Moon. "I wish we could ride after him and make sure he's all right," Sam said.

"We could, if we knew where that trail led." Brynna pointed to the exit from the canyon.

"Maybe you could see it on the map. I've only been up here a few times, and it's like a maze," Sam said.

Across the canyon, the Phantom returned to his perch. His battle won, his herd safe, he flowed up the switchbacks and through the clumps of brush to the place where he kept watch.

"Ready to head back?" Brynna asked.

"Sure," Sam said. Although she would gladly sit and watch the Phantom all day, Ace shifted restlessly beneath her. "I think Ace is getting cold and I don't want his legs to stiffen up."

The horses tackled the path back up with leaps that made Sam worry about falling backward out of the saddle. She lowered her chest against Ace's neck and felt relieved when they reached the even footing of the main trail through Lost Canyon.

The trip out of the canyon seemed quick, and Sam's mind was racing on ahead, thinking of the algebra homework she still had to do, and the timeline she needed to make for history.

Someday she might learn not to leave her homework for Sunday afternoon, but someday wasn't now. Besides that, she hadn't folded laundry like Gram had asked her to the other day. Gram had said she could either wear her clothes wrinkled or get out the ironing board.

She'd just about given up on having any fun for the last hours of the weekend when she spotted Moon.

"Look who's here," Brynna said.

The young black stallion had waded into the center of the lake on War Drum Flats.

"He *is* a beauty." Sam sighed.

Moon stood about fifteen hands tall, but the smooth line of his back and the gentle slope of his shoulder and his long graceful neck made him appear even taller.

Without leaving the water, he turned his face toward Ace and Jeep. He sighed and tossed his head, but the gesture was no challenge.

His heavy black mane was ragged where the Phantom had ripped it. His neck and hindquarters showed slashes. When he stamped, the knee he raised was scuffed pink. He looked altogether crestfallen and confused.

Sam rubbed Ace's neck as she talked to Brynna. "Moon doesn't know whether to welcome these guys or try to run them off."

"I think he'd welcome his bachelor band about now," Brynna said. "Have you seen any sign of them lately?"

"No," Sam said. "We can ask Mrs. Coley, but how would that help? I can't tell Moon how to find them."

Ace started forward, but Sam tightened her reins. "No, you can drink at home. Leave him alone to figure out what happened."

As they headed past the lake toward River Bend, Sam couldn't help looking back.

Moon gazed after them, but he still stood in the muddy little lake.

Driven out of his family, unable to find his friends, the lone mustang would have to figure out where he belonged. Sam felt a tug of sympathy.

Then she looked ahead, watching for the familiar silhouette of River Bend Ranch to appear on the horizon.

She felt sorry for Moon, all right, but he wasn't the only one whose world was about to change.

Chapter Six

Sam smelled apple pie baking as soon as she and Brynna rode into the ranch yard. The aromas of cinnamon and pastry made her instantly hungry.

"Oh, my gosh. I hope that's for us," Sam said.

"Why wouldn't it be?" Brynna asked, laughing.

"Because Gram has a habit of baking delicious treats, then giving them away." Sam's stomach growled.

Gram came out on the porch just as Sam finished speaking.

"One of them's for us," Gram assured her. She wiped her hands on her apron. "The other is for Brynna to take home."

"Why can't she stay for dinner?" Sam asked, surprised to realize she really wanted Brynna to stay.

"I wish she would," Gram said. "Before you two even left, she told me she had to get home and do paperwork." Gram turned toward Brynna. "Couldn't you change your mind?"

Brynna rubbed Jeep's shoulder as she shook her head. "I'd really like to, but the report's due tomorrow. I've been working on it for weeks." Brynna's expression turned self-mocking as Sam's dad walked toward them from the barn. "It seems like something keeps distracting me."

"Can't imagine what that could be," Dad said. His smile was white in his darkly tanned face.

Sam searched her feelings for jealousy and found only a tiny crumb. She was starting to like Brynna.

Dad stood at Jeep's head, preparing to steady Brynna as she swung down from the saddle, then he kissed her.

"You guys are embarrassing me," Sam said. Dismounting from Ace, she felt her cheeks heat in a blush.

Dad and Brynna laughed.

"Spare yourself by moseyin' down to the barn and putting up Ace and Jeep," Dad said.

Sam didn't protest, just took the reins Brynna held out to her.

"Thanks." Brynna gave Sam a quick hug. "I really do have to work on that report. It wouldn't be a good idea to lose my job before we're even married."

"That wouldn't bother me much," Dad said.

Sam bit her lip to keep from asking what the heck Dad meant. Between drought and flood, River Bend Ranch was often short of money. Dad had even sold his horse, Banjo, to help make up losses. Brynna's income from the Bureau of Land Management would be a big help.

Brynna tucked a wisp of hair back toward her braid, then stood a little straighter. She drew a breath as if she were about to say something, then didn't.

"No dating service would match up a cattle rancher and a lady from BLM, I bet," Sam said. She was joking, but she knew Dad's and Brynna's differences would spark some lively arguments.

"We're working on that," Brynna said.

"Lucky we met the old-fashioned way," Dad said at the same time.

Sam remembered how irritated she'd been the day Dad and Brynna had met up at Willow Springs. From the first, Dad's scorn for the BLM hadn't tainted his attraction to Brynna. He'd been amused by her attempts to talk him into adopting a wild horse.

"She may not be working forever," Gram said. "For the BLM or anyone else."

Gram's tone was sly. Could she be hinting that Dad and Brynna might have a baby?

Sam's stomach flipped over. Having Brynna move into the house was one thing, but becoming a big sister while she was in high school was something else.

"I wish," Brynna said, as Sam braced herself, "that the HARP program would be approved and I'd be hired to manage it."

"That would be kind of cool," Sam said.

The Horse and Rider Protection program matched

abused mustangs with at-risk girls. Mikki Small, the first to try out the program in Nevada, had worked with the albino mustang Popcorn at River Bend.

Mikki had started out as a rude, destructive kid with a record of breaking the law. Popcorn had been "shown who's boss" far too often before he was taken away from his adoptive family. But anyone who'd seen Mikki bid farewell to the shy albino would know the program had worked miracles.

"When will we know if the program's approved?" Sam asked.

"We're supposed to know before Christmas," Brynna said.

"My report went in months ago and they've interviewed Mikki and her social worker."

Dad gave a satisfied nod. "Both of them had good things to say, I figure."

"That's what I hear," Brynna said. She held up both hands with fingers crossed, then prepared to go. "Thanks again, Sam, for riding out with me. I'll keep watch for Moon."

Half an hour later, Sam had cooled out the two geldings, curried them, and checked their feet for pebbles. Ace was in his corral rubbing necks with Sweetheart, and Sam was leading Jeep to the ten-acre pasture, when a battered green camper pulled into the ranch yard.

Jeep's steps skittered nervously at the barks coming from the camper, and Blaze dashed growling across the yard. He'd allowed the truck to pull in, unannounced, because he recognized it.

So did Sam.

Jen Kenworthy, her best friend, sat in the truck's cab next to her father, Jed. Two years ago, the Kenworthys had been forced to sell their ranch to Linc Slocum, but Jed had stayed on as foreman. In that time, Jed had done a lot of unusual stuff for Slocum, but Sam couldn't imagine why he'd be hauling a load of dogs.

Sam hurried Jeep through the pasture gate. As soon as she released him, he joined the other saddle horses, who stood snorting their interest from a safe distance.

Blaze wasn't as cautious. The black-and-white Border collie jumped up, trying to see through the camper windows.

Toenails scrabbled on metal and furry bodies rocked the camper. The barking never stopped. Inside the cab, Sam could see Jen pressing her palms over her ears.

"Blaze, you've got no sense at all," Dad said as he strode toward the dog. "You can't take on a whole pack."

He grabbed Blaze's collar and led the protesting dog to the kitchen door.

"Sorry," he shouted as he closed the dog inside.

Sam didn't think Gram was going to enjoy Blaze's company.

Jen slipped out of the truck, hands still covering her ears. Sam smiled as Jen reeled toward her, black-framed glasses askew.

Finally freed from the skirts and twin-set sweaters her mom had made her wear before freshman year, Jen's clothes expressed her individuality. Today she looked like a walking harvest fair.

She wore an orange-and-yellow plaid sweater, red corduroy jeans, and black high-top tennis shoes. The ends of her white-blond braids were bound with some kind of fuzzy little pumpkins.

"Save me," Jen croaked as she staggered closer to Sam.

"What's with all the dogs?" Sam asked.

"Another one of Slocum's grand ideas," Jen moaned.

Linc Slocum was always dreaming up schemes to make him look like a real Westerner. His ideas weren't always harmless. He'd had a rustler capture the Phantom, then tried to adopt him. He'd bought Brahma bulls and tried to show them off through Karla Starr's illegal rodeo shows. Luckily, his ignorance often made him fail.

Over her friend's shoulder, Sam saw Dad talking to Jed Kenworthy. Jed might be Linc Slocum's foreman, but here at River Bend, he was his own man.

Jed and Dad looked alike. Both wore faded jeans and shirts with metal snaps. Tanned, scarred hands hung at their sides. Both looked down, and both seemed amused and disgusted by their conversation.

"What now?" Sam asked.

"Rented lion hounds," Jen said.

Lion hounds. Sam felt uneasy as Jen rattled on. That had to mean Slocum planned to hunt down and kill the cougars.

"And that's not all. We had to drive into Reno to pick up some gear that's so high-tech even *I* don't understand how it works. And you know how I love electronic stuff."

Sam did. Jen was a math and science whiz. For fun she puzzled out bizarre equations and programmed her computer to do amazing things.

Together, the girls walked closer to listen to their fathers' conversation.

"It was just bad luck this turned out to be lion season. Slocum's got his hunting license. That cost him less than fifty bucks, but he's in Reno buying a new truck to go huntin' in. And this pack of hounds he's renting didn't come cheap. Their daily rate would make a normal man's heart stop." Jed Kenworthy rubbed his hand across his lips as if he wanted to erase what he'd just said.

"I didn't know you could rent dogs," Dad said, sounding as if he couldn't imagine a bigger waste of money.

"They're not just any dogs." Jed's response accompanied a lopsided smile. "They have electronic tracking collars, and we have to tote a black box full of computer gadgets, so that if the hounds take off after something we can figure out where they've gone."

"I bet Linc won't be the one toting that box," Dad said sympathetically.

"Heck no, and it can do more than track the dogs, too. Did I mention it makes sounds like a dying rabbit or a deer in distress? These were his second choices, though. What he really wanted was to do an aircraft flyby, then get some night-vision goggles and—"

"Mr. Kenworthy," Sam interrupted. She heard her voice quaver and she steadied it. "Have you talked to Jake Ely about the cougars?"

"No," Jed said, eyebrows raised. "Should I have?"

"Jake says the tracks show the mother is limping and she's just teaching her kitten how to hunt."

"That so?" Jed shook his head. "Might be some point to this after all, then. An injured cougar is more likely to take down unusual prey. Instead of waiting for a deer or antelope, she'll take whatever she can. Like a horse and rider."

Both fathers looked at Jen and Sam. The girls rode together in desolate areas all the time.

Sam had the awful feeling she'd just made things worse, so she gave Dad a look that begged for help. She wasn't sure he even noticed.

"You taking Sundance up there after a cat?" Dad jerked his head toward the ridge as if he couldn't believe Jed would put his palomino Quarter horse in such danger.

"With those hounds drooling around his knees? Don't think so." Jed shook his head. "That's a lot to ask of any horse, if he's not trained to it. Especially if we get one."

He was talking about shooting a cougar and bringing it out dead. Sam didn't want to picture it, but the image filled her mind. To a horse, the cat would look and smell almost alive. Few would tolerate the limp weight of a cougar swaying over their withers.

"Why doesn't he hire a guide and do it right, since he's set on doing it?" Dad asked.

"Doesn't want a guide taking credit for the kill." Jed looked through the camper window. A swarm of speckled dog faces greeted him. One even licked the glass.

"He wants it for a trophy?" Dad glanced back at the house as Blaze renewed his barking.

"Sorta," Jed said. "He wants a hide to tack up on the side of the barn."

Sam gasped, then reminded herself she was not going to act like a kid anymore. She could hide her feelings, but right now it was hard. With a half-hearted wave, she jogged toward the barn.

That poor injured mother cougar. She was only teaching her baby to hunt so he could do it for himself. The cub would have to learn or starve. Why would Slocum want to make that cub an orphan?

Sam grabbed the barn doorway. Inside, she heard straw rustle. She walked toward the warmth of resting horses. Overhead, a pigeon cooed in the rafters. Outside, the men laughed. Sam bit the inside of her cheek. Once she was alone with Ace, she could cry if she had to. But she wasn't alone. She heard Jen's steps coming up behind her.

"Are you okay?" Jen asked.

"I can't believe," Sam said slowly, "your dad is going out there with Slocum."

"He doesn't want to," Jen answered.

"But he's going to do it anyway."

"He's been thinking about what's the best thing to do. It's not an easy choice, Sam." Jen sounded reasonable, but Sam could tell she didn't like defending her father. "He figures he can either let Linc go out alone, get mauled, and have the ranch sold off to someone who won't let us live there," Jen explained, "or he can go help him and get it over with."

"But it's wrong," Sam insisted. "Those cats haven't hurt anybody."

Jen took her time retying the ends of her braids before she answered. "You're probably right. So maybe my dad should just let Linc go out there alone, and maybe the cougars would get away. That'd be nice. But what if Linc wounds one of them? You know he'd just leave it out there, suffering. Then what?"

Sam didn't know. Right and wrong shouldn't be this complicated.

"I'll tell you what." Jen's voice rose louder with each word. "Then my dad would have to go out and shoot it *again*."

Wings flapped. A disturbed pigeon swooped down from the rafters and flew out the barn door.

Silence settled around them. Sam walked farther into the barn. Ace slung his head over the top of his corral and nickered.

"But he's joking about it," Sam said, letting Ace whuffle his lips across her palm.

"Well, your dad isn't exactly horrified."

Sam knew Jen was right. Standing together, the two ranchers had been twins in their looks and in their acceptance of the cougars' death sentence.

"But my dad's not going out with Slocum."

"Do you think my dad likes it? Do you think *I* like it?"

"Then—"

"We both like it more than leaving the ranch!" Jen shouted, then she waved her hand at Sam, dismissing her. "Sometimes you really are a city girl. Maybe when you grow up, you'll see not all decisions are easy. Not everything's black and white."

Jen stormed out of the barn.

Sam sat in the clean straw outside Ace's pen and listened to the horse move around. She answered him each time his nicker asked what she was doing.

"I'm still here, Ace. Still trying to learn to keep my mouth shut and my feelings to myself. I can't even tell my best friend what I'm thinking."

Sam pulled her legs up against her chest and clamped her arms around them. She rested her chin on the shelf they made and listened. She didn't leave the safety of the barn until she heard the green camper bumping away, across the River Bend bridge, and dusk had fallen, turning everything a hazy shade of gray.

Chapter Seven

Sam's guilty conscience woke her at four A.M.

It was stupid, and she knew it, but what else could it be? She'd mistreated her best friend. Not accidentally, but on purpose. That's what had her staring toward her ceiling when it was still too dark to see.

She'd finished her homework last night, so school worries weren't keeping her awake.

She hadn't had a bad dream, though thoughts of Moon, injured and alone, and the about-to-be-orphaned cougar were nightmarish enough.

She wasn't cold. She didn't have sore muscles or a cough or a headache to keep her from sleeping until her alarm clicked on at six o'clock.

Nothing was wrong except that she had only three hours to decide how she'd face Jen at the bus stop and apologize. The worst part was, Sam wasn't sorry.

Sure, she regretted their quarrel, but she still thought Jen's dad was wrong. The cougars shouldn't have to die and Jed Kenworthy shouldn't help Slocum kill them.

Sam rolled onto her stomach. She closed her eyes and tried to kick free of the sheet wrapping her like a mummy. If she kept thrashing around, she'd wake Gram or Dad and then she'd have another set of problems.

She sat up carefully, hoping her mattress wouldn't creak. She wiggled her feet free, then tiptoed across her room to pull on jeans, a flannel shirt, and heavy socks. She laced on her gym shoes and started downstairs, where she put on her coat.

The only one who'd welcome her at this time of the morning was Ace. And, she admitted to herself, even that was iffy.

As Sam left the house and closed the door quietly behind her, she decided to stop by the feed room and get a scoop of grain, just in case.

Ace nickered before she reached the barn, and though Sweetheart snorted and turned her tail toward Sam, the little bay gelding *was* happy to see her.

"Hey, pretty boy," she whispered.

Ace nickered again as she entered his pen.

Long ago, Jake had told her it just made sense to pet horses in the same places they groomed each other, and he was right. As Sam rubbed Ace's neck, the horse sighed with pleasure.

"So, Ace, do you think I'm a city girl?"

Ace stamped one hoof.

"I don't think so, either. I only spent two years in San Francisco. Jen knows the numbers don't support what she's saying, so why would she say it?"

Ace shifted his weight toward Sam. She rubbed harder.

"And she told me to grow up." Sam paused as Ace shook his mane. "Okay, something like that. And I'll tell you the truth, Ace, I don't want to ask her what she meant."

Sam worked her fingers through the gelding's coarse black mane. "Know what I think? That I should save those cougars myself before Linc has a chance to kill them." Sam let her words hang for a moment. "I should do it myself," she repeated, as if trying to convince herself it was the right thing to do.

At the bus stop, she and Jen would make up. None of their squabbles lasted longer than overnight. After each of them apologized, she'd ask Jen to meet her after school. Together, they'd ride the ridgeline, looking for cougar tracks. When they found the mother and cub, they'd bother them a little. Not enough to terrify them, but just ride after them a little and hope the cats took off for the high country.

Slocum wasn't likely to follow the cats into bleak, snowy terrain where the riding was cold and difficult.

All at once, Sam felt sleepy. It just figured. She'd

only been out of bed about fifteen minutes and her body had decided it was nap time. If she hurried, maybe she could catch more sleep before her alarm rang.

"'Bye, boy." Sam kissed Ace on the nose, slipped out of his pen, and jogged toward the house.

Before she was halfway there, a commotion of clucks and a flurry of feathers erupted inside the chicken house.

Sam stopped. What was that? She peered toward the coop. Had something moved?

No other animal was inside the chicken house now, or the hens would still be squawking, but she'd seen something like a wave of black near the fenced chicken yard.

Sam continued cautiously. If she were a horse, a dog, or almost anything but a human, she'd have better night vision. She opened her eyes as wide as possible, then squinted. Nothing was there.

Keeping a watch over her shoulder, Sam continued toward the house. As soon as she opened the door, the kitchen light came on. Sam jumped back. Of course, it was just Gram, wearing a red robe zipped up to her neck, looking at Sam in surprise.

"Good morning!" Gram said as she flicked on the oven. "You startled me." She ran water into the coffeepot, set it to heat, then asked, "Is everything all right?"

"Fine," Sam said. There was no sense mentioning

the turmoil in the chicken house. "I just couldn't sleep."

"Hmm," Gram said. "I wonder why."

Sam noticed Gram hadn't really *asked* why. Still, Sam sagged into a chair instead of going upstairs. Her eyelids were heavy, but she couldn't help but watch as Gram darted around.

Gram opened the refrigerator, removed two pans of bread dough that she'd left rising overnight, and slipped them into the oven. They'd be baked and ready for butter and honey at six-twenty, the time Sam usually came down for breakfast. Sam wished they were ready now.

Next, Gram ground coffee beans in a hand mill and poured them into the old tin coffeepot. Finally, she made Sam's lunch and slipped it into the back-pack Sam left hanging by the door.

By then the coffee was ready. Gram poured her-self a cup, sipped it, then tilted her head while she looked at Sam.

"I know it's not your usual, but what about a cup of coffee with lots of cream and sugar, and maybe a piece of apple pie?"

"Oh, yes." Sam practically growled the words. Last night, after her fight with Jen, she hadn't been hungry for much dinner.

Smiling, Gram cut two triangles of pie. She gave Sam a pink pottery mug of pale coffee, then sat down across from her. Just then the heater came on, filling the kitchen with warmth.

"You didn't have any pie last night," Gram observed.

Sam sipped, giving herself time to think. Why shouldn't she tell Gram what had happened? She couldn't come up with a single reason.

"Jen called me a city girl and told me to grow up."

"She did?" Gram's eyebrows rose. "Now, I wonder what made her do that."

"Am I?" Sam asked. "And aren't I pretty mature for thirteen?"

"I think you're a grown-up thirteen," Gram said. "But Jen's more adult than you." Gram raised one hand to stifle Sam's protest. "She's had to be, dear. It was very hard for that family when they lost the ranch." Gram stirred her coffee, though she'd already drunk half of it. "I don't think I'd be telling tales if I said that living under Linc Slocum's thumb has caused problems in Jed and Lila's marriage. On the other hand, Wyatt and I have protected you from everything we could."

"Like what?" Sam asked.

"Oh, money troubles, our little spats, conflicts between the cowboys . . . " Gram's voice trailed off, then she met Sam's eyes. "So, yes, I'd say Jen's had to be more grown up."

Gram was distracted by sudden clucking outside. "Is Blaze bothering those hens? He hasn't been himself since Jed brought those hounds over."

"I think Blaze is in the bunkhouse. I didn't see

him." Sam wished she had. Something was sniffing around the chicken coop, and Blaze would have flushed it out of hiding.

Sam's fork cut through the lattice crust of her pie. The first bite tasted so good, she didn't want to ask about Jen's "city girl" remark, but Gram hadn't forgotten.

"While I don't think anyone's justified in calling you a city girl, it's not such a bad thing. I wish—" Gram gave a sigh, took off her wire-framed glasses, and rubbed the bridge of her nose. "I do so wish you could have seen your mother the first day she came to this ranch."

"*She* was a city girl," Sam said. "I know that."

"Oh, she was. Her makeup was perfect and her hair curved just so. She had manicured nails, too. Louise was as citified as they come, but it was love at first sight when she set eyes on River Bend.

"Your father met her in college, of course. He thought she just liked the idea of ranch life, so when he brought her out here, it was sort of a test."

"That's not very nice," Sam said.

"Not very," Gram agreed. "But Wyatt had a hard time believing she was real."

"I don't understand."

"Well, you might have noticed that ranch folks hide their feelings some. Happy, sad, or mad, we don't make a scene." Gram let her words sink in, as if she knew Sam had been thinking of this very thing.

"But Louise . . ." Gram tsked her tongue, smiling. "That girl always wore her heart on her sleeve, and Wyatt just didn't know what to make of it."

"But she passed Dad's test."

"Land, yes. They hadn't even gotten out of his car when Wyatt's old dog, Trixy, came streaking across the yard with a face full of porcupine quills."

"Oh, no!" Sam couldn't keep her hands from flying up to cover her nose and mouth. "Dogs have such tender noses, too."

Gram nodded. "Your father didn't bother calling the vet. Not because he was cruel, mind you, but because it was the third time Trixy had pulled that stunt."

"And she got quills in her face every time?" Sam gasped in disbelief.

Gram grimaced and nodded. "Even inside her mouth."

"Why didn't she learn?"

"Who knows? But this was the last time she did it. In minutes, your mother, in her pretty blue dress and sandals, was helping Wyatt tend Trixy." Gram stared at the kitchen wall as if it showed a film of that day. "Wyatt held that big brown dog between his knees, keeping her still. Louise used pliers to jerk those quills out, while tears ran down her cheeks. She was so softhearted, but she was tough, too. She pulled every one of those quills.

"And when they were all finished and Trixy came over and licked your mother's face? She fell on her knees and hugged that dog until Wyatt didn't know what to do.

"From that day on, Trixy was as much Louise's dog as she was Wyatt's. More than once, I heard him joke that he only married Louise to please Trixy. Yes, I imagine you're a lot like your mom was at your age. She was a city girl, but she wasn't squeamish. She did what had to be done."

Sam and Gram finished eating with only the refrigerator's hum to fill the quiet. Upstairs, Sam's clock radio started playing and Dad's feet hit his bedroom floor with a thump.

"I better go brush my hair," Sam said.

"Could you collect eggs for me first, since you're already down here?" Gram had gotten up to peek at her bread, so she didn't see Sam wince. "Your father's not much for pie-and-coffee breakfasts, and he might as well have his eggs fresh."

"Okay," Sam said. She took a basket from the kitchen counter and turned on the porch light before she went outside.

The night had faded to gray and the Calico Mountains were outlined purple against the horizon, but Sam felt nervous approaching the chicken coop.

Why didn't one of the cowboys open the bunkhouse door and let Blaze out? The hands were always up by now. Maybe they were eating breakfast, but if she could hear the dog scratching the door, so should they.

Then, when she was just a few yards from the chicken coop, Sam heard something else. A movement like a big snake, or a thick rope being whipped across the ground. She'd never heard the sound before. She froze, staring through the chicken wire at something dark hiding on the other side.

The porch light reflected in two large amber eyes.

It's not a big animal, Sam told herself as she studied the white-rimmed mouth that was open, but very low to the ground.

Across the yard, the bunkhouse door opened.

"Go on then, you crazy cur." Pepper's voice was muffled by a yawn, but Blaze leaped from the doorway, flying over the wooden stairs. The dog hit the ground running.

Sam heard a low yowl and knew what she'd been watching, and what had been watching her. A cougar.

Should she shout and try to scare it away? Should she tackle Blaze and try to keep him from being hurt?

Too late. Dirt spat from beneath huge padded paws and the yellow eyes vanished. But Blaze followed right behind.

"Blaze!" Sam shouted. "Come back here!"

Dad was on the porch, making a whistle more shrill than anything Sam had ever heard that early in the morning.

It worked.

Sneezing the dust from his nose, trotting as if he'd filled his paws with stickers from the cold morning ground, Blaze came back and picked his way toward the porch.

"What's got into that dog?" Pepper called from the bunkhouse.

"I don't know," Sam yelled back.

She hated lying, but she would not give anyone a reason to hunt down that cougar and orphan its kitten.

She took a deep, steadying breath and opened the chicken yard gate. Her hands shook as she gathered the eggs. There weren't many. Had the cougar been skulking about all night, making the hens too nervous to lay?

When she'd searched all the nests and come up with only three eggs, Sam quit looking.

She opened the gate and headed back toward the house, then noticed Dad was still standing on the front porch. He petted Blaze in an absentminded way, and he kept staring toward the ridge.

Chapter Eight

Gram's Buick slid up to the bus stop with just minutes to spare. Sam climbed out of the car, took a deep breath of the icy air, and got ready to apologize, but Jen didn't look up.

Was she really searching for something in her backpack, or just pretending? Sam couldn't tell, but Jen didn't shift her attention until the bus stopped and opened its door.

Then, she rushed ahead and took their usual seat.

"Cool sweatshirt," Sam said, sliding in beside her. "Did you tie-dye it yourself?"

"My aunt did it," Jen muttered. "About a hundred years ago." Her answer was better than a simple no, Sam decided, but Jen just stared out the bus window after that.

"See anything?" Sam asked finally. "Llamas, flying squirrels, alien aircraft?"

Jen turned from the window, but she pressed her

spine against the seat back and still didn't look at Sam. From the side she looked pale, and there were gray smudges under her eyes, as if she hadn't slept.

"I'm not ready to make up," Jen said. "My dad may be a jerk, but he's still my dad."

"I know," Sam began.

"No, you don't. You have no idea." Jen's voice was cold, brittle, and completely unlike her.

Tears pricked the corners of Sam's eyes, but Gram had just finished telling her that ranch folk hid their feelings. Sam lifted her chin and cleared her throat. She refused to cry on the bus, where everyone would see her.

When Jen gave a sigh, the sound might have been the opening of a valve releasing the pressure from inside Sam's own chest.

"I'm not going to be mad forever," Jen said, sneaking a quick glance at Sam. "But please don't make me talk."

"Okay," Sam said.

She tried to think of something else for the length of the ride. She slid her fingers through her hair, trying to improve the shape of the caplike cut Brynna had given her the night before school started.

She really needed to get it trimmed. Any other morning, she'd convince Jen they needed to make a trip to the Crane Crossing mall. There had to be a cheap stylist there, but today the idea seemed too frivolous to discuss.

And asking Jen to go look for the cougar was definitely out. Sam knew she'd have to revise her plan, but she wasn't sure how until the bus arrived at Darton High School.

Sam and Jen parted without promises to meet at lunch. They gave silent waves and hurried across the parking lot toward class.

Sam had almost made it to the school building when she saw a familiar blue pickup truck pull into a parking spot.

It was like a clown car, Sam thought. How many Ely boys could actually fit inside and in the truck bed? They spilled out, all with black hair and blue jeans. Sam stood still, waiting in the cold shadow of the building.

When Jake walked within range, she'd pounce. Here he came, dressed just like the others, except for his scuffed brown leather jacket.

Jake scoffed at most of her plans, but he was just as worried about the cougars as she was. If she presented this problem the right way, Sam knew she could make him go with her after school.

Wait, he must have seen her. Why else would Jake have changed direction and headed for the front of the building rather than entering the door closest to his locker?

"As if you're going to escape," Sam muttered.

She pushed through the door and rushed toward Jake's locker. Even though he had longer legs, she could be there waiting when he arrived. If she hurried.

Sam dodged elbows and backpacks. She didn't look at her watch for fear she'd see how little time remained before the first bell rang.

She wanted to go to her own locker, too, to drop off some of the books weighing her down. But that could wait until she'd extracted a promise from Jake.

Mr. Blair stepped into the hall just in front of his classroom door, blocking Sam's way.

She'd never beat Jake now. But Mr. Blair was her journalism teacher and advisor to the school newspaper, the Darton *Dialogue*. And Mr. Blair was a big guy. He stopped traffic so effectively, he might have been a brick wall.

"Forster," he boomed.

Mr. Blair extended a raggedly opened letter toward her. Behind him, Sam saw RJay, editor of the *Dialogue*.

Sam took the letter. She didn't want to look at it. There was still time to find Jake, but RJay was already announcing what was inside the envelope, so Sam didn't have much choice. She had to look.

"Second place," RJay told her. "You got second place in the Night Magic contest."

Sam skimmed the letter. Two teachers — Mr. Blair and Mrs. Ely — had encouraged her to enter the photo contest. After her success in photographing Hammer, the stallion who'd challenged the Phantom,

Sam had been eager to enter. She'd almost missed the deadline, though, after all the turmoil over the mustangs slated to be destroyed.

Finally a photograph had just presented itself while she was holding the camera. When Sam mailed it in, she'd been proud.

The picture showed Jake with Faith, a foal owned by Trudy Allen, the owner of a neighboring ranch.

Faith was blind, and she'd wandered off in the midst of a snowstorm. Sam had been among those searching for Faith, but she hadn't been the first to find her. The lucky little filly couldn't have known that a guardian angel, in the form of the Phantom, would herd her toward a hot springs and watch over her.

After riding for hours, Sam had found Faith. When Jake had come along, they'd decided he should carry the foal home across the withers of his mare, Witch. It was snowing hard and Jake had looked like a tender grizzly bear, burly but careful as he scooped up the filly and carried her. Sam had been holding her camera. One touch of her finger and she'd had the picture.

While Sam was remembering, RJay and Mr. Blair were arguing.

"She should've earned first prize," RJay insisted.

"She should've focused," Mr. Blair contradicted him. Then he waved aside RJay's annoyance.

"Besides, she's just a freshman, and she earned a gold-edged certificate."

"With that and a buck, she can get a tuna sandwich in the cafeteria," RJay snarled.

Boy, you could get away with a lot if you were the editor, Sam thought. The bell rang, covering Mr. Blair's response, but he didn't look too annoyed.

Rather than jump into a discussion that would probably go on without her, Sam shoved the letter back into its envelope and detoured around Mr. Blair and RJay.

"Thanks!" she shouted. "See you after lunch."

Then, with no time to take her books to her locker, Sam ran for her history class. And she made it.

During the daily announcements over the school intercom, Sam heard there was a math club meeting during lunch. Jen always attended, so Sam wasn't surprised to be eating lunch alone.

She munched an apple and decided it was okay if Jen got a little more time to think things over. Besides, Sam had a meeting of her own to arrange.

She ambled toward a hidden position outside the cafeteria and waited. This time, Jake wouldn't escape.

He and his friends were creatures of habit. Every day they gobbled lunch, then left the cafeteria in a group. Obnoxious Darrell always led the pack, while Jake, the quietest in his rowdy crew, always exited last.

There went Darrell, jeans flapping. Next came

Jake's brother Brian. Then a few other guys, but no Jake.

Sam had followed the group only a few steps when Darrell spotted her. "No need to stalk me, Sam," Darrell said, loudly enough that heads turned. "Just say the word, and I'm yours!"

"In your dreams," Sam said, but she could feel the heat of a blush. "I'm looking for Jake."

"Check over your shoulder, honey." Darrell leered and pointed.

Sam whirled. Jake was right behind her. His leather jacket was open over his white tee-shirt. Though his black Shoshone mane was tied back with its usual leather shoelace, he looked different today.

Sam couldn't figure out what had changed. Was he standing taller? Holding his head a little higher? Whatever. She wasn't here to analyze his appearance.

"I need you to go ride with me after school," Sam blurted, "and help me track the cougars up on the ridge."

"Help *you* track the cougars?"

"Well, I tracked one of them to our chicken coop this morning," Sam said. That was almost the truth, although a witness might argue over who was tracking and who was hunting.

"Yeah?" Jake asked, sounding lazy.

Sam folded her arms. It was risky trying to wait Jake out. On the range, he'd stay silent for hours, but sometimes at school he got restless before she did.

Sam watched a boy quarreling with his girlfriend.

She watched a puzzled gull circle over the rally court. Then she studied a crack in the sidewalk where one hardy weed was still sort of green.

This time, Jake's patience broke first.

"Why do you want to go following them?" he asked.

Sam wanted to applaud herself, but she didn't.

"To scare them off so Slocum won't find them and shoot them."

"Doesn't sound smart, scaring animals that can swipe the horse right out from under you and have it for dinner. What's the point?"

Sam glared at Jake. He was annoyed that she'd outwaited him, so he said something like that. But she didn't give up.

"The point is, Slocum has a pack of lion hounds, a bunch of electronic tracking equipment, and . . ." Sam let her voice trail off when Jake began rubbing the back of his neck.

He and Dad both did that when they were uneasy.

Quit while you're ahead, Sam told herself.

"All that stuff for one injured cat," Jake mused, looking down at his feet.

He seemed to be thinking something over. His stillness reminded Sam of what Nate had told her. Jake had been bothered by a dream he'd had, a dream about cougars.

He should ask his grandfather to explain the dream, Sam thought. Jake joked that the old man lived in the past, but he was a tribal elder and a respected interpreter of spirit dreams.

"Are you going to call your grandfather about your dream?" Sam braced herself for Jake's temper.

"I already talked to him."

Sam swallowed. "You did? You actually called him and asked him about your dream?"

Jake's wooden expression softened into something that might have been amusement or wonder. "No, he called and asked *me* about it."

Sam licked her lips and tried to think of something to say. She couldn't, so she took advantage of Jake's attention.

"After school, tell me about what he said, okay?" she asked.

"Don't know why you have to be so pushy." Jake still looked unsure. "Think you're goin' alone, if I don't go with you?"

"Of course I am."

"Not if I tell Wyatt." Jake didn't sound protective. He sounded like a ten-year-old tattletale.

"Jake," Sam said, rolling her eyes in impatience. "Haven't we outgrown that?"

Sam realized they'd been standing in the hall talking an awfully long time. Darrell and the others had gone off somewhere and the bell was about to ring.

"Please, Jake. It will be more fun with two of us. And safer," she admitted.

He made a grumbling sound, then pointed his index finger at her. "Four o'clock at the trailhead behind your place. Be there and ride . . . " Jake shook his head. "Shoot, I wish Ace was bigger, but yeah, ride him. We won't have long."

Sam nodded, but she didn't understand why Jake was fussing about Ace's size and the amount of time they'd be riding.

"No way am I keeping you out after dusk," Jake added. "That's when cougars get hungry and serious about hunting."

At three forty-five that afternoon, Sam was ready to leave River Bend. She'd rushed through her after-school chores, promised Gram she'd do homework right after dinner, then hurried to saddle Ace.

As the mustang watched Sam, his black-edged ears tipped and swiveled to each sound she made. He seemed annoyed by her nervousness.

When Sam adjusted his bit for a second time, making sure it sat in his mouth so he'd feel her slightest signal, Ace nuzzled her.

"Are you telling me to lighten up? Hmmm, boy?" Sam tried to laugh at herself, but she couldn't help stepping back to slide her hand under Ace's cinch.

The latigo strap that held the saddle in place lay smooth and flat. Ace hadn't pulled his old trick of holding his breath, then letting out air so the cinch swung loose.

Actually, he hadn't tried that stunt for a long time, but this would be a bad time to make a mistake.

Sam slid her boot into the stirrup and swung up, letting her weight test the saddle's position. Then she threw her right leg over and settled in.

"I don't know why I'm so worried," she told Ace. "You've probably seen lots of cougars."

Sam rode through the old pasture and let Ace step over the downed fence rails. She kept watch on the faded sagebrush around her and aimed Ace toward the trailhead. She'd heard cougars loved the meat of young foals. Sam closed her eyes, but the awful images wouldn't vanish.

She wanted to believe the Phantom's watchful, protective mares wouldn't give cougars a chance to snatch their babies, but she knew it could happen.

The cougars had to be chased away, for their own safety and the safety of the wild horses.

Ace would be a big help today. He'd lived free. Before he was captured by the BLM, he must have seen mountain lions and come to know them as enemies. He would scent the big tawny cats before Sam saw one.

Still, she kept looking. The trail went weaving up the hillside, past boulders and brush. A cougar could be hiding anywhere. What sounded like wind rustling through branches could be a cougar gathering itself to pounce.

Why had she pictured the cougars running away from her? They were predators. Horses—with or without riders—were their prey.

Chapter Nine

*A*ce tossed his head high and wheeled hard right, back the way they'd come.

Sam slipped in the saddle, but she couldn't fall. Not now, with cougars on the prowl. She forced her weight back toward center, righting herself in the saddle as Ace uttered a long whinny.

Sam didn't have time to be mad at him before realizing the sound was a greeting, not a warning.

"Hey, Brat."

The voice made Sam relax. No one except Jake used that silly nickname. Right now, she'd tolerate it without complaining. If she was riding into danger, there was no one she'd rather have beside her than Jake.

An instant later, he rode out of a copse of cottonwoods, black Stetson pulled low on his brow, barely moving with the jog of his black mare, Witch.

Witch gave a snort of recognition. In the cold, the

breath jetting from her nostrils looked like smoke. The roached-maned mare surged forward like a black dragon.

Ace gave a hop and a squeal of pleasure. Even as Sam waved at Jake, she thought Ace might be excited to see Witch for the same reason she was pleased to see Jake. They both hoped there was safety in numbers.

"See any mountain lions on your way over?" Sam called. She tried to sound casual, so Jake wouldn't know she was afraid.

The part of the ridge Sam knew best ran behind Jake's family's Three Ponies Ranch, behind River Bend, and on past Linc Slocum's Gold Dust Ranch. It offered about twelve miles of easy access to all three ranches and their livestock. If she were an injured cougar, she'd use it instead of roaming over the range.

Jake shook his head, not speaking until Ace and Witch fell into step. "No. A few tracks and signs, though. They were headed this way when I lost them."

Jake leaned right, then left, checking the ground as they rode. Witch was used to his weight shifting in the saddle, but Ace shied.

Sam snugged her reins and let Jake ride ahead. If there were cat tracks along this ridge, she didn't want to trample them.

"Let's try Aspen Creek," Jake said. "The altitude's lower, it's warmer, and mule deer go there to water. Those things oughta attract the cats." He didn't sound convinced.

"Why are you worried?" Sam asked.

"Whatever's wrong with the mom cat, she's getting worse. Instead of limping, she's dragging the injured paw. It's on a hind leg, and she needs both hind legs to hunt."

"I thought cougars got up in trees and dropped down on their prey."

"Sometimes, but look around." Jake gestured at the terrain. "The trees are bare and there aren't any cliffs. That's why I want to go down by Aspen Creek, where there are still trees with leaves."

Oh good, Sam thought, *so they can drop down on us*.

"What about that?" Sam pointed at an overhanging shelf of old snow.

"That's just left over from the last storm," Jake said. "It doesn't look too stable to me. I bet if you rode up there, it would break right off."

After a closer look, Sam decided Jake was probably right. But then she thought of this morning.

"But the cougars were down by our chicken coop," Sam told him. "I know that's what I saw."

"I believe you," Jake said. "But a healthy cougar can travel twenty-five miles a day, and it's only three or four miles from here to River Bend." Jake shrugged. "That's not good news that they were down by the house," he added. "She's already shown her cub how to wait in the brush. He doesn't need to practice that. Wait. Stalk. Act." Jake emphasized the words as if they were a process all mountain lions memorized. "They should be working on step three. A cougar as big as this one shouldn't be hoping to catch a hen."

"How old do you think her cub is?"

"At least a year," Jake said, and Sam knew his certainty came from the size of the cougar's paws. "He's big, but inexperienced. She should be teaching him how to rush a deer before it scents him. He's big enough to spring on a deer's back and still keep his hind legs on the ground for stability."

Sam pictured that kind of attack. It would be like the attack of a rearing stallion—only with teeth and claws.

"Good-sized cats like this one have been known to kill even bears that way," Jake said, "with a single bite on the neck."

Instinctively, Sam hunched her shoulders and glanced around. "What kind of tracks are we looking for?"

"I'll take care of finding tracks. You look for scrapes and scratches."

Sam tried to understand exactly what he meant. Jake must have seen her confusion.

"Scrapes are piles of dirt kicked up by a cat's hind feet. And you know how house cats tackle a scratching post? They mark trees the same way, reaching high up and pulling their claws down like they were ripping your sofa."

"We've never had a house cat," Sam admitted.

"Just barn cats and they're pretty wild."

"You're joking." Jake's smile said he couldn't believe he wouldn't know this about her. "Mom's calico is about to have a litter—want a kitten?"

"Dad doesn't like cats," Sam said.

"What about Brynna?" Jake asked cautiously.

Sam felt a glow of appreciation for Jake. Because he valued his own privacy, he was careful with hers. "You know they're getting married, right?"

"Clara and her waitresses aren't much for keeping secrets," Jake said.

Sam thought that over for a second. If the waitresses at Clara's diner were serving this gossip along with coffee and cake, everyone in the area must already know about Dad and Brynna.

It surprised Sam that she didn't really care.

"I don't know if Brynna likes cats, but I know everything's going to be different." Sam considered one of the white-trunked aspens alongside the trail. Those weren't gouges, just dark marks on the pale bark.

"Maybe some of it will be good different," Jake said.

"Maybe," Sam said. "But what if I want to do my homework in front of the TV, and she tells me to go up to my room? Or if I go into the tack room to talk to Dad and she interrupts? And even if she doesn't, I'll be talking to him, just knowing that she could show up any time she feels like it."

"Yeah," Jake said. "You know, my dad's talking about having my grandfather move in with us."

"But he's cool," Sam said.

"How do you know?"

"I met him at a rodeo once, and that's what I've heard." Sam didn't remind Jake that most of what she'd heard had been from his own mouth. "Please tell me what he said about your dream."

Jake laid his hand on Witch's neck as if she'd trembled.

"Not that much."

"I won't stop asking," Sam warned, "so you might as well tell me now."

"There's not much to tell. He said cougar dreams are about coming into your own power," Jake spoke in a half-mocking tone, but Sam noticed the way he squared his shoulders and lifted his chin. *That's* how he'd seemed different this morning. He'd looked more powerful. More like a grown-up. "About leadership and self-confidence. It doesn't take a—" He shook his head, and Sam noticed his long hair was tucked up under the Stetson. "Look, that's stuff you could tell any guy my age and be pretty close to right."

Jake paused, and Sam knew there was more to his grandfather's dream translation.

"What else?" Sam asked.

When Jake refused to answer, Sam leaned forward. She was ready to harass him more when Witch jumped sideways with a sharp grunt.

Wait. Stalk. *Act.*

Sam turned quickly in the saddle, searching right, left, sure she'd see a feline shape bounding toward them. She stayed low on Ace's neck and firmed her legs around him. Just ahead, Jake allowed his body to follow Witch's movements.

Sam saw no cat.

"It's okay, boy," Sam murmured, though Ace knew best whether he had a reason to be afraid.

"Shoulda seen that comin'," Jake snapped as Witch returned to a jittery walk.

Sam could tell he was scolding himself, not his horse.

"Seen what? Was it that?" Sam pointed at a branch no bigger than her arm. It lay beside the trail, gold leaves fluttering.

"Yeah. But they're expecting the worst. There must be cat smell all over."

Ace lifted his hooves like a parade horse as he passed the branch. Eyes rolling to show some white, he remained watchful, just in case.

Ten minutes later, both horses stopped, nostrils testing the air as the trail dipped toward Aspen Creek. Even Sam could smell the difference.

Snow had fallen recently, but the valley still looked like fall and the breeze smelled like apple cider. It flowed through the gold haze of pollen hanging in the air. It fluttered the yellow leaves, making them applaud other leaves floating like sailboats on the small creek.

Then there was a splash.

Round rocks rolled, and a black mustang walked down the creek to give a snort of challenge.

"Moon!" Sam gasped. She turned to Jake, but he was frowning.

His eyes ran over Moon with such concentration, Sam wondered what he was trying to figure out.

"Blackie's herd?" he asked, under his breath.

"Yes."

Once, the Phantom had been known as Blackie. He'd been born on River Bend Ranch, son to two captive mustangs named Kitty and Smoke. Sam had raised the colt by hand, and when Jake had helped her train him to saddle, he'd still been called Blackie.

Months ago, Mrs. Coley had spotted Moon running with two other bachelor stallions. She'd called him New Moon, because he was night black and had no white markings at all. Neither had Blackie.

Jake considered Moon as if the horse was a ghost. Sam knew he still felt guilty over the accident that had made her fall from Blackie, suffer a concussion, and leave River Bend for a long recovery in San Francisco.

Sam wanted to shake him and say it *still* wasn't his fault. He wore a protective look as he turned to her, but Sam cut him off before he could say a word.

"Blackie's son," Sam whispered. "His name is New Moon."

That quickly, Jake's expression changed. He gave her a disgusted look. He thought it was wrong to name wild things.

"His dad tear him up like that, do you think?" Jake muttered.

"Yes," Sam said.

Dark red bites marked Moon's rump and neck. His mane was ragged where the Phantom had grabbed and pulled.

When Ace and Witch answered his snort, Moon forgot his challenge. He leaped onto the bank and trotted closer.

He needs a herd, Sam thought. Moon tossed his forelock away from his hopeful eyes. He was drawn by the two horses, even if he feared their riders.

Then, as if a door in his memory had opened, the mustang slid to a stop. Did he remember the rustlers who'd caught him, herded him into a truck, and kept him prisoner until Brynna had him released?

Moon turned, galloped back up the riverbank, then vanished among the trees.

"He's a beauty," Jake agreed before Sam could ask.

"Brynna and I saw him fight with the Phantom the other day when we went into Lost Canyon."

"Thanks for telling me all about it," Jake muttered.

"That's not fair," Sam said. "You won't even talk with me, half the time."

"This is the other half," Jake explained. "When

you have something worth sayin', I'm all ears."

Sam shook her head at Jake's contrariness, then told him about the stallions' fight and Brynna's concern that the Phantom's herd was on Indian land.

"Don't know nothin' about that," Jake said.

"I didn't expect you to. Brynna will look it up on a map."

"I do know there's some other property in dispute," he said. "Dad said Slocum was complaining that some of what we fenced for Mrs. Allen belongs to him."

"What?" Sam thought of the hours she, Jake, and his brothers had spent working with wire and fence posts. "He can't take back the mustang sanctuary. Not even part of it." But she knew Mrs. Allen had sold some of her property to Slocum. "Can he?"

Jake wasn't listening.

"There," he said, pointing at a patch of riverbank where brush crowded near the water.

Sam saw only one cougar print. To her, it looked like an impression made by a dog's paw, though the toes might be rounder and more widespread.

Feeling her rider's excitement, Witch trotted up the bank as Jake leaned from the saddle. His lips moved. He read the prints as if they were words.

At last he looked up, but his triumphant expression had vanished. Jake's jaw was set hard. He looked angry.

"Tell me what kind of equipment Slocum has

again," he ordered.

"He has dogs with electronic tracking collars, and a recorder that plays the sound of a distressed deer or rabbit, and—"

"Not floodlights? Jed Kenworthy didn't mention night gear?"

"Yes, he did," Sam said. "But he told Dad that Slocum couldn't use any because—wait. He said something about only being able to hunt mountain lions during the first half hour before sunrise and the first half hour after sunset."

Jake nodded. His gaze swept the silent clearing around them. "Maybe they'll be all right, then," he said. "I sure hope so, 'cause those cougars are headed toward Gold Dust Ranch."

Chapter Ten

Maybe Miss Finch was psychic.

Sam's English teacher had assigned a poem that made her think Miss Finch knew about the mountain lions.

Sam sat cross-legged on her bed. She'd written the answers to the questions that followed the poem. Her other homework was finished and she was already wearing her nightgown. Still, she sat up, reading the poem once more.

Tyger! Tyger! burning bright
In the forest of the night . . .

The poem gave her shivers. The words created a picture that could have been drawn from the cougar eyes she'd seen by the chicken coop that morning.

Sam stared at the reflection of her bedside lamp on the dark glass of her window and remembered how the front porch light had made those cougar eyes smolder like golden coals.

How much scarier would it be to see those eyes gleaming back at you if you were Jake, alone by a campfire?

Sam rubbed the gooseflesh from her arms and told herself to squash her imagination. Jake was smart. He was home, safe and warm. Although he'd asked about Slocum's gear, and clearly was worried that the rich rancher would go lion hunting at night, Jake wouldn't ride through the dark to Gold Dust Ranch, trying to save those cougars.

Should she phone him to be sure?

No. Jake knew the animals' best chance would be their own instincts. The cats would hear Slocum from miles away, and run. If they could.

Sam closed her book and crawled into bed. She turned off the light and tried not to think of Jed Kenworthy's reaction when she'd said one of the cats was injured. That had solidified his decision to help Slocum hunt the cats. Jake seemed worried about the injury, too. He blamed the mother's wounded paw for the cats' nearness to civilization.

Jed and Jake could be right. It must be easier for a cougar to catch unwary house pets or livestock than wild deer.

Sam pulled the covers up to her nose. It would be cozy to have one of Mrs. Ely's kittens curled up, purring, beside her. Maybe she'd ask Dad tomorrow.

She sighed, closed her eyes, and smiled. Then again, she just might ask Brynna instead.

Sam's dreams were crowded with cats.

Mostly cougars, she thought, as she got dressed for school. In one nightmare, though, her calf, Buddy, had been running with Moon. Both had fled a yellow kitten with oversized fangs. Though the dream was silly, a feeling of dread still hung over Sam after breakfast.

When Gram's car reached the bus stop, Jen seemed glad to see Sam. She was walking toward the Buick before the big car had even rolled to a stop.

Jen's puffy pink parka was pulled up to touch her matching ear muffs, and she rubbed her mittened hands together. She was biting her lip so hard, she seemed more worried than cold.

Gram must have thought the same, because when Sam opened the car door to get out, Gram leaned forward.

"Is something wrong, dear?" she called to Jen.

Outside, Sam stood beside her friend. Jen shifted from foot to foot.

"Not really," Jen said. She used the back of one mitten to push her dark-framed glasses up her nose. "Linc and my dad went out hunting before dawn. There were kind of a lot of gunshots, and, you know, it's a little creepy."

Sam moved closer to Jen, until they stood

shoulder-to-shoulder. Without saying a word, she told Jen she knew exactly how she felt.

Gram shook her head in a way that was not sympathetic. "Land, I thought there was really something wrong," Gram scolded. "I'm surprised at you, Jennifer. You, too, Sam. If you plan to be ranch women, you'll have to get used to this sort of thing. Injured animals have to be destroyed. Tame animals have to be protected from wild ones. It's part of ranching."

Sam wanted to blurt out the ugly truth: Slocum wasn't protecting his livestock, he was after a cougar's skin he could show off on the side of his barn. But Sam kept quiet, afraid Jen might take her words as more criticism.

"Have a good day at school, now," Gram said when neither girl answered. "And don't worry about things you can't change."

Sam closed the car door. Gram drove off and Sam stared after her, feeling angry.

If killing innocent animals was what it took to be a ranch woman, maybe she didn't belong here, after all.

Sam let the thought simmer as her eyes lifted to the Calico Mountains. Their peaks were frosted with apricot snow, colored by the rising sun. Up there, the mustangs might be waking and pawing the ice from clumps of grass.

"I think Gram's wrong," Sam said to Jen. "There can be all kinds of ranch women, even ones who love wild horses and feel sorry for cougars."

Before Jen answered, they both turned toward the sound of an approaching engine. It came from the wrong direction to be the bus, and it was too early for Mrs. Coley, the Slocums' housekeeper, to be driving Rachel to school. Besides, it sounded like a truck.

A champagne-colored Jeep Cherokee, windshield wipers twitching away the frost, came down the road from the Gold Dust Ranch.

"Slocum's new hunting truck."

Sam was pretty sure that's what Jen had said, but her friend's lips sounded numb.

Keep going, Sam thought, willing the truck to drive past, but Slocum's toothpaste commercial grin showed through the windshield and the Cherokee was slowing.

Sam looked down the highway, wishing the bus would arrive before Slocum did, but she knew that wouldn't happen.

"I don't want to talk to him," Sam said.

"Then don't." Jen tucked a mittened hand around Sam's arm and squeezed. "He's so wrapped up in himself, he'll never notice."

Jen was right.

Slocum stopped on the highway in the exact spot the bus would occupy any minute. Careless of the fact that he was parked the wrong way in a traffic lane, he rolled from the vehicle and hustled around to the back doors, which were right in front of Jen and Sam.

"Y'gotta see," he huffed. "Before I take her into the taxidermist. Don't want her stuffed, you know, but the hide has to be tanned so it looks good on the barn."

Sam felt as if her chest were hollow and each of Slocum's awful comments echoed in the emptiness. He had one of the cougars in there.

Slocum jiggled the handle on the back of the Cherokee.

Don't open, she thought. *Let it be stuck.*

But it wasn't. It took Slocum a minute because he was unfamiliar with the latch holding the doors closed, but finally he got them open.

Eager and smiling, Slocum looked at the girls over his shoulder.

"Well, c'mon, take a peek." He stood, hands on hips, regarding the blanket-wrapped bundle. "Cost me a pretty penny, this cat—what with the hounds and truck, and all—but I can afford it, and she'll look good when I get her fixed up."

Sam's head swam. She'd never really seen the cougar alive, but how could Slocum think she'd be more beautiful dead?

At last, Slocum seemed to realize he was the only one admiring the cougar. As his grin turned into something greedier and more ugly, Jen managed to speak.

"Is it the mother or the cub?" she asked.

"The female," Slocum said. "She came in alone,

ahead of the dogs. Guess she stashed the yearling someplace." Slocum shrugged, then whipped aside the blanket.

Sam tried not to look. She'd already had her share of nightmares.

Blood spots marked the blanket. Sam noticed that detail before she realized both she and Jen had covered their lips and wondered what they were keeping inside.

"No more appreciation than I expected," Slocum muttered as he slammed the doors. "Like to see either of you do what I did." Jen uttered a small sound of protest, then closed her lips again.

How weird was this man? Sam wondered. Why was he taunting two high school kids?

Still, neither Sam nor Jen answered his dare.

The Elys' faded blue truck zoomed past on the highway, carrying Jake and his brothers to school. Slocum watched them grow smaller, then sneered at Sam.

"You be sure and tell your boy Jake that he did the right thing by staying out of my way. He may be a big tracker, but I'm the one who brought home the bacon."

As Slocum returned to his truck, Sam shook her head. *Bringing home the bacon,* Slocum had said, when he had a dead mountain lion in his truck. The tangle of words should have been funny, but they weren't.

Dizziness kept Sam from closing her eyes, though

she wanted to block out what she'd seen. Between the time Slocum had pulled the blanket aside and the moment Sam had looked away, she'd glimpsed the cougar's face.

The animal's pink nose had looked heart shaped. Around it, a line of black hairs might have been painted by an artist's brush. Whiskers sprouted from puffs of white fur, and a pink tongue hung from the cat's mouth. Above all those features, the cougar's eyes were brown and dull.

Tyger! Tyger! burning bright . . . Sam thought. *Not anymore.*

All during that blustery day, Sam's steps dragged as she moved from class to class. She wished she were home at the kitchen table, drinking hot chocolate.

It was cold, but the temperature hadn't dropped enough to turn the blowing rain to snow. Sam thought of how miserable the young cougar must be, alone and wondering what had become of his mother. She thought of Moon, wandering without the warmth and safety of the herd.

In the middle of her P.E. class, while they played freeze tag in the gym, Sam stood like a statue, hoping Moon and the young cougar wouldn't face each other as enemies.

Sam and Jen ate their lunches without mentioning Slocum, the cougar, or Jed Kenworthy's part in the hunt.

In fact, the lunch hour passed quietly, until Jen said, "Rachel told me you went with her to look at horses."

"Yeah," Sam said. "There's one she really liked, a Morgan named Mocha, over at Sterling Stables."

"I'm surprised you went with her." Jen crumpled up her brown bag loudly.

Sam didn't want to admit how out of place she'd felt and how angry she'd been at herself for going along.

"Yeah," Sam said again.

"I've got to get to class." Jen swung away from the table, stood, and strode off toward her locker.

To Sam, Jen seemed mad again, but it had been such a lousy day, she might just be turning paranoid.

Sam hurried to her own locker, pulled out a purple notebook, then slammed the metal door.

Just one more class, Sam thought as she made her way through the tide of students toward journalism.

"I need a volunteer," Mr. Blair was shouting as Sam walked into the room.

She slipped toward the computer farthest from the teacher, even though that meant sitting near Rachel.

From Rachel's whispers to her cheerleader friend Daisy, Sam learned that the staff photographer scheduled to shoot the football game after school was sick. Daisy thought the photographer was faking.

Sam considered the slushy rain pelting the windows. It would be convenient to come down with a cold about now.

She glanced up and saw Mr. Blair's eyes scanning the classroom. Sam curled over the keyboard, typing nothing in particular. The last thing she needed was an after-school photo assignment.

"Forster," Mr. Blair bellowed.

"She's back here." Rachel raised her hand in a dainty pointing motion.

"I take the bus," Sam shouted back. She tried to infuse her voice with a little regret, but Mr. Blair ignored her excuse.

"You're good at shooting in low light, and if this slush turns to blowing snow, that's what you'll have out there."

Wind could get up a lot of force, rushing across the broad football field. Sam hated the idea of standing out there, shivering.

"I don't have a ride home," Sam protested.

"No problem. I'm staying for the game," RJay told her, then raised his voice. "Mr. Blair, I'll give her a ride."

"Why don't you shoot it? Please, RJay," Sam begged.

"Me? I'm not an award-winning photographer. Sam, you'll get something great. I know it."

"I'm not that good. I only took second place," she reminded him.

"You were robbed," RJay insisted. "Besides, when your editor and your advisor say you're shooting a game, you shoot it."

"Or flunk," Rachel chimed in.

Sam hid by bending down to tie her shoelaces. She should've worn something besides these lightweight hiking boots. They'd turn soggy right away. She jerked the knot tight, to keep them from filling with snow, and the right lace broke. Looking at the scrap in her hand, Sam decided that some days were simply cursed.

She arrived home after dark.

The heater in RJay's car hadn't worked well enough to thaw Sam's frozen toes. Her teeth were chattering as she came into the warm house.

"I'm home," she managed to announce.

A television babbled from the living room. No one came to greet her, and she could see Gram had already served dinner and cleaned up.

"I'm starving," she shouted.

"I left a plate for you," Gram called.

Sam opened the oven to see a white china plate crowded with meat loaf, carrots, and mashed potatoes, which reminded her just a little too much of the snow starting to mound up outside.

The door between the kitchen and living room opened just as Sam slid her fingers into an oven mitt and reached for her plate. "How was the game?" Dad asked.

"We lost in double overtime," Sam said.

"Too bad." Dad closed the oven. "Before you sit

down, could you make one turn around the yard? Your Gram's short a hen, and she's been out three times since sundown looking for that one Rhode Island Red."

"Sure," Sam said.

She pulled her coat closer, switched on the porch light, and walked outside. The snow had stopped and so had the wind. The sky was cloudless, black, and sprinkled with stars.

"Here, chick, chick, chick," Sam called. Nothing moved around her. Even the hens in the coop didn't flutter.

Where was Blaze?

Sam didn't like being out alone. She trudged through the snow and her boots left ridged patterns, showing her where she'd been. She circled the coop, walked as far as the barn, and stood in the warm straw.

"Hi, Ace," she said, answering the gelding's nicker. "Seen any runaway hens?"

If he had, Ace wasn't telling. Sam looped through the old pasture, looked up at the ridge, then shivered all over again.

"Too bad, henny penny," she muttered. "It's going to be a long, cold night."

Sam turned back the way she'd come, ready for dinner. She'd only taken a few steps when she looked down—and stopped. She took a deep breath, then started jogging toward the front porch light.

She ran a zigzag pattern. She flapped her arms and sang "Jingle Bells" as loud as she could. Anyone who saw her would think she was crazy, and Sam didn't care. She was still yards from the front porch when she jumped—and made it.

She wrapped her arms around her ribs and stared into the darkness. Blaze wasn't out there, but she hadn't been alone.

All the way back to the house she'd followed her own footprints in the snow. Inside them, tracking her out to the barn and through the old pasture, she'd seen the soft padded print of a mountain lion.

Chapter Eleven

Sam rushed inside. Her hands were cold and clumsy as she hung her coat. She stared at the brown leather and swallowed hard. Head down, walking into the wind, had she looked like a deer to the young cougar?

It was her warmest coat, but she wouldn't wear it around the ranch for a while. She hoped she wouldn't have to explain to Gram and Dad.

"You can bring your plate in here, Samantha," Gram called from the living room.

"That's okay," Sam said, searching for a quick excuse. "I'm going to study while I eat."

Sam didn't want to hurt Gram's feelings, but she didn't want to talk about what it took to be a ranch woman, either. Not now.

The yearling cougar had come to River Bend with his mother. He'd learned he could find food here, and he'd probably eaten the hen.

Would the cougar still be hungry? How much would it take to satisfy his appetite? Could he eat a lone horse like Moon, who didn't have the protection of a herd?

Dad might know. Or Jake. She had to ask one of them, and soon. The young cougar was getting brave.

Sam had finished her meal when she heard floorboards creak overhead. The sound was followed by the click of Blaze's toenails as he came downstairs. Sam heard him start to whine.

She opened the door between the living room and kitchen and let him through.

"And where were you when I needed a bodyguard?" she whispered.

The Border collie gave Sam a brief wave of his tail. Then he stood with ears pricked, staring as if he could see through the wall.

Just as Sam started to worry, Blaze lost interest in whatever he'd heard. He flopped down on the floor and rested his head on his front paws. He seemed to doze, but his ears stayed alert.

Sam opened her algebra book and considered the single index card her teacher had said they could use for notes on tomorrow's quiz. She'd need more than this puny white piece of paper to record what she had to remember from this chapter.

"How was that meat loaf?" Gram called.

"Really good," Sam answered. "And the mashed potatoes were perfect."

She should go in and talk with Gram and Dad, but the football game had cut into her study time. She didn't want to walk through the living room and take the chance of being distracted by the television.

Blaze growled so suddenly, Sam jumped. The rumble grew deeper and more vicious as the dog rose to his feet.

"Blaze, hush," Sam said.

The dog's fur stood up across his shoulders and his lips drew back to show his teeth. It had to be the cougar.

"You're not going out," she whispered to the dog, but he ignored her.

Even if the young cat was inept and Blaze was furious, the dog would be hurt. If Blaze was in danger, Dad would protect him. Dad's rifle was in a locked case in the living room, but he could have it out and loaded in seconds.

Blaze gave one loud bark, then subsided into growls again.

"He sounds serious," Gram said. Sam thought she was talking to Dad.

"Blaze!" Sam's voice couldn't cut through the sudden volley of barks or the lunge against the kitchen door. Dad's feet hit the floor in the other room.

"What in the—" Dad's single stride took him halfway across the kitchen floor.

Sam stepped in front of the kitchen door. "Don't let him out!"

"Why not?" Dad's voice was low, but she heard him over Blaze's barks.

Sam couldn't let it happen. There'd be a whirling tumble of fur and teeth and one of the animals would probably die.

"Samantha?" Dad's voice said she'd better speak up, right now.

"I think it's the cougar."

Gram was in the kitchen now. "Linc shot—"

"It's the other one," Sam interrupted. "The baby."

Dad gave a quick nod. He switched on the porch light. Just as he slipped past Blaze and stepped outside, Sam heard a ringing impact. Something big had hit the wire around the chicken coop.

"Wyatt!" Gram shouted.

Blaze bounded back and forth in front of the door, then jumped, trying to see from the window.

Sam peered out, but the angle was wrong for her to see the coop. What she could see was Dad waving his arms.

"Get out of here!" he shouted. "Go on, now!"

Blaze's barking stopped and Sam could hear Dallas call from the bunkhouse.

"What ya got out there, Boss?"

Dad shouted something back, but because he was facing the other direction, Sam couldn't tell what he said.

"Should we send Blaze to see him off?" Dallas yelled.

At the sound of his name, the dog barked again.

"No, I think we've seen the last of him," Dad said.

Gram had crowded beside Sam at the window. They watched Dad leave the porch and walk across the ranch yard to meet Dallas.

As the men talked, Gram turned to Sam and asked, "You're sure it was the cougar?"

"No. Maybe—it could have been a coyote."

"Not likely. They're awfully quiet, but a young cat who didn't know what he was doing . . . Throwing himself against the wire is just the sort of thing he'd do."

Sam saw Pepper leave the bunkhouse and cross the yard with a flashlight. He swept the beam around the chicken coop. When he called out, Dad and Dallas walked over to join him.

After all the nodding and pointing, Sam knew they'd seen the tracks of the mountain lion.

"It's nine o'clock," Gram said. "You'd better start getting ready for bed."

"Please, not yet," Sam said. "I've got to talk with Dad."

"I'm afraid you won't like what he has to say," Gram warned. "And I don't know why you've gotten attached to these dangerous animals. They could kill any one of us, and that includes the horses. Thank goodness Dark Sunshine isn't due to foal yet."

Gram was right, but Sam had to explain her feelings.

"Linc Slocum only killed that cougar so that he

could hang its skin on his barn," Sam blurted. "He orphaned that cub for no good reason. Linc created the problem, but the cub has to pay for it."

She'd heard Dad come back into the house while she was talking. She turned to look at him. Though he leaned down to rumple Blaze's ears and praise him, Dad kept his eyes on Sam.

"Was it the cat?" Gram asked.

"Yeah, and since we've never had trouble with one before, I'm pretty sure it's the one Sam was talking about." Dad's eyes were sympathetic, but his voice wasn't. "I'll give him a day or two to head up into the mountains."

Sam didn't want to ask the question, but she had to.

"What if he doesn't go?"

"That chicken won't fill him up for long," Dad said. "He needs a deer a week — or prey that amounts to that many calories. If he doesn't get it, he'll get too weak to hunt and he'll starve."

"Could they trap him and take him somewhere with other cougars?"

"They're solitary animals, Sam. Far as I know, they only get together in mating season."

"When is that?"

Dad rubbed the back of his neck and frowned. "Seems like I've seen pictures of them together in winter, but I'm no expert."

"Okay." Sam stood looking at the floor until the wood planking began to swim before her eyes. "I guess I should go to bed."

All at once, Sam wanted to hurry. Something in the way Dad shifted his feet made her suspect something worse was coming.

"Sam?" Dad's voice stopped her. "I'll give him two or three days, *if* no one gets hurt. If he shows up near the house again, or attacks a horse, or claws a River Bend calf out on the range, the deal is off."

When Sam and Jen got off the bus after school the next day, Sam felt their fight was almost forgotten. She was still careful not to mention the cougar or Jen's dad, but she'd quit weighing her words.

Now, as the bus pulled away, they stood talking before starting their walks home.

"I'll be calling you about my algebra. I don't get polynomials at all," Sam moaned. "And I can't believe it's only Tuesday."

"It's a challenge fit for Einstein," Jen agreed. "The week that never ends."

Sam laughed in bewilderment. Jen was always saying things like that, as if she had a crush on the dead scientist. Sam promised herself that someday she'd learn what all the fuss was about.

"Although maybe," Jen mused, "I shouldn't hope it does."

"Shouldn't hope the week ends? Why?"

"Because Princess Rachel will be ruling Gold Dust Ranch for a week."

Sam recoiled. "Where's Linc going?" she asked.

It wasn't as if Rachel would have much to do. Mrs. Coley managed the house and Jed Kenworthy ran the ranch. Nothing was likely to go terribly wrong. Still, handing Rachel any control was frightening.

"New York. To meet Ryan."

"Ryan? Rachel's twin?"

"That's the one," Jen said. "I guess Linc's combining a business trip with meeting Ryan at the airport when he flies in from London."

So that's why Rachel had dragged her off horse shopping, Sam thought. Ryan lived in England with their mother and he was a serious horseman. Rachel wanted to dazzle him with her new horse. Except she didn't have one.

"Was your grandmother supposed to pick you up for something?" Jen asked, shading her eyes as Gram's Buick rolled toward them.

It turned out that Jen's mom had called to say Jen could go riding with Sam without coming home first. Gram looked a little nervous as she explained.

"Since you two are of a size and Sam has plenty of riding clothes, I thought that would be fine," Gram said.

For a few seconds, Jen looked confused. Then her expression turned to hurt.

"That means my parents are fighting again," she mumbled to Sam as they climbed into Gram's backseat. "And they don't want me around."

Sam felt awful, but Jen sounded so certain. There was no point in trying to convince her that she was wrong. Sam decided she would try a different approach to cheer Jen up.

"Who do you want to ride?" she offered. "Pick any horse on the place."

"Wow." Jen rubbed her hands together and gave a wiggle of delight as if her parents' problems were forgotten. "Even Popcorn?"

"Especially Popcorn," Sam said. Jen was a good rider, so whatever choice she made would be perfect. "Brynna said HARP probably won't get up and going until at least spring break. We don't want Popcorn to forget everything he's learned."

Once they reached River Bend, the girls ran upstairs, changed into riding clothes, and talked about where they'd go.

"We could go toward War Drum Flats," Jen said. "But if there are mustangs at the water hole, it might be hard for Popcorn."

"Yeah, if he saw a whole herd, he might want to join them," Sam said. Then she thought of something that would really please Jen. "You know what, though? I can't promise he's still there, but if he is, I'll show you a really neat mustang. He's alone, so I think Popcorn will do fine."

Jen looked dubious. "You expect him to be where you last saw him?"

"He's sort of a special case," Sam explained.

"Just trust me, okay?"

The girls hurried downstairs.

"Gram, is it all right if we ride over to Mrs. Allen's and see how Faith is doing?" Sam asked. Aspen Creek was hardly out of the way. The detour wouldn't take more than an extra twenty minutes.

"I suppose that would be all right," Gram said, but she looked uneasy. "You girls stay together, now."

When Gram or Dad said that, Sam wondered if she should explain that she and Jen went riding or to the mall because they liked to do things together. *Why would we split up?* Sam wanted to ask. But she didn't.

"We will," she said instead.

Sam brushed Ace and saddled him while Jen stood in the big pasture with Popcorn.

When Sam returned, leading Ace and carrying a brush and the tack Jen would need, the albino mustang was still sniffing Jen over.

Nostrils flaring, Popcorn checked the hand Jen held out for his inspection, then whuffled his lips over the end of one braid and finally nuzzled the top of her head.

"Do I pass, boy?" Jen asked quietly.

Popcorn looked away as if he were bored, and Sam decided he no longer considered Jen a threat.

"Okay, I think you can tack him up," Sam said.

"I'm going to spend a little time grooming him," Jen said.

"He could use it," Sam said. Rolling in the mud was an unfortunate habit for a white horse, but Popcorn loved it.

"Not only that," Jen said, "but I was reading that since horses in the wild scratch each other's backs and whisk flies from each other's faces, they consider you a member of their herd if you do the same."

It made sense, Sam thought, so she tried to be patient. She rode Ace up and down the fence, making him turn with quick precision, until Popcorn was brushed and saddled, and Jen had mounted.

Clumps of mud flew up from Ace's hind feet as he bolted in front of Popcorn.

"Hey," Sam scolded, but Ace didn't take her reprimand to heart.

Though he was at least a hand shorter than Popcorn, Ace held his head high. Then, when the albino tried to catch up, Ace flashed his teeth.

"Since when do you want to lead the way?" Sam asked, shortening her reins.

"Maybe the cold weather makes him frisky," Jen said. Then she dipped an arm as if bowing. "After you, my dear Ace."

They'd ridden over the bridge and started along the far side of La Charla, toward a group of grazing Herefords, when Jen's conversation circled back to the Slocums.

"Can you believe that when Linc meets Ryan, he's bringing him a new car? And then they're going to drive across the country together?"

"If he's even half as spoiled as Rachel, I can believe it," Sam said.

Jen fixed Sam with a strange look, then shook her head.

"What?" Sam asked.

"Nothing." Jen rode in silence for a few steps. "Do you remember one of those days when Mrs. Coley gave us a ride home with Rachel?"

"After I got kicked off the bus," Sam supplied. Although that memory wasn't one of her favorites, she hadn't forgotten.

"Right. Well, one of those days, Rachel told us that Ryan was the conscience of the family."

"I remember," Sam said, though she couldn't figure out why Jen was still frowning at her. "But I'll believe he's a great guy when I see it for myself. Two out of two members I've met from the Slocum family are creeps."

"Whatever!" Jen shouted, suddenly angry. Popcorn's pace faltered.

"What?" Sam said, surprised by Jen's outburst.

"How can you call Rachel spoiled and creepy when you're hanging out with her?"

"Are you crazy?" Sam squawked.

Sam had to shift her attention as Ace tugged at the bit. Maybe the gelding didn't like the shouting. Maybe he thought the cattle up ahead needed herding. Either way, Sam knew if she didn't pay attention, and quick, he might misbehave for real.

"Shhh, boy," Sam said. As she smoothed her hand along Ace's neck, Sam realized what Jen meant.

Still, she gave her friend a minute to settle Popcorn. The albino seemed to trot on tiptoe, and his ears flicked toward Ace. If the bay was worried, he figured he should be, too. When both horses had calmed down, Sam took a deep breath.

"I'm not hanging out with Rachel," she insisted. "I did go horse shopping with her. She wants one that'll impress Ryan."

"So you spent the day with her," Jen said. "And the difference between that and hanging out is . . ."

Sam sighed. Maybe Jen was extra sensitive because her parents were fighting. If so, Sam figured she could be extra patient.

"The difference is, although I looked at a bunch of cool horses with Rachel, I had a lousy time. I felt ugly and out of place and I couldn't *wait* to get away from her."

Sam saw Jen hide a smug smile.

"In fact," she continued, "I purposely got Rachel to ditch me at the Elys' place, and Gram picked me up. Driving all over the county with Rachel is torture.

"This," Sam said as the horses swung into an easy lope, "is hanging out."

Jen smiled, and Sam returned her attention to Ace. The bay gelding was still skittish, and Sam became so focused on him that Jen's sudden comment puzzled her.

"This was a bad idea, after all," Jen muttered. She hauled her reins in tight, but Popcorn bowed his neck and made a low, rumbling nicker.

When Sam looked ahead, she saw a dozen mustangs mixed among the grazing Herefords. She recognized the Phantom's tiger dun lead mare, and then she saw the silver stallion himself.

Fierce and fiery as a knight's charger, the Phantom moved down the bank of La Charla, preparing to confront another stallion.

Chapter Twelve

"It's Yellowtail," Sam whispered as the chestnut stallion approached from upriver.

It would be exciting to watch this confrontation between stallions, but Sam knew that if they'd kept to her plan to drop by Mrs. Allen's ranch, then cross back over the river to Aspen Creek, Popcorn wouldn't be acting as if he'd never heard of a saddle.

Jen fought to keep the white gelding under control. Finally, she turned his head toward his tail. When he got dizzy from spinning, he planted all four hooves and trembled, watching the mustangs ahead.

"Good work," Sam said, but Jen brushed off her admiration with a shake of her head.

"Are you sure it's Yellowtail?" Jen asked. "It's been months since we saw that bachelor band."

"It's him," Sam said.

Flaxen mane and tail shining in the November sun, the chestnut and his two mares picked their way toward the river.

"I've been thinking about that band a lot," Sam added, "because Moon was with them."

"The black horse you think is the Phantom's son?"

"Yep. He's the mustang I'm taking you to see in Aspen Creek after we visit Mrs. Allen."

All at once Sam shivered. She shaded her eyes and scanned the surrounding terrain, looking for Moon. Aspen Creek canyon was only a few miles downriver. If Moon showed up here now, it could mean trouble. The Phantom was already insulted at Yellowtail's approach. Adding another stallion to the mix would be bad news.

But she saw no sign of the black, so Sam turned back to watch Yellowtail face the Phantom.

The silver stallion glanced at her and flicked his ears in recognition. Then he faced the intruder, and the Phantom's manner changed.

Neck and tail arched proudly, he vibrated with fury. Maybe he couldn't believe Yellowtail had invaded this riverbank pasture.

"This isn't his usual place," Sam said. "But he acts like it's his kingdom. Look at him."

Though they were no closer than if they'd been seated in bleachers, watching a football game, the sound of snorting stallions made it seem a little too close.

"He acts like this is his turf, all right," Jen murmured in agreement. "I've read that mustangs aren't territorial, but . . ." Jen was still puzzling this out when the stallions bumped noses, shook their heads, then rose on their hind legs. "Oh, watch out!"

The stallions reared for only an instant. Next, they whirled and lashed out with their heels. For a few kicks, they fought as equals, but then the chestnut stumbled and the Phantom's neck curved. Mouth open, he lunged for Yellowtail's forelegs.

The chestnut regained his feet and sidestepped. Unsteady but determined, he stood between his mares and the Phantom.

"I don't think the Phantom wants Yellowtail around his herd," Jen said. "What do you think?"

"It looks that way," Sam agreed.

Yellowtail trotted farther off, but his thirsty mares were still headed toward the river.

With a squeal, Yellowtail blocked them.

"Isn't that just like a guy?" Jen pointed as the chestnut clacked his teeth, threatening his mares. "He's taking his embarrassment out on them."

Sam's laugh froze as all the horses tossed their heads high and pricked their ears. A long, joyous neigh pealed through the air.

"Is that Moon?" Jen asked.

It was. The black stallion looked carefree as he leaped from the river to the bank and shook. Still wet with river water, he galloped toward the other horses. Cattle scattered as Sam worried for the young stallion. Didn't he know that both herds would reject him?

Moon approached at a weaving lope.

"He's acting like it's a game." Sam heard her own dread.

"No," Jen said. "I think he's unsure of how they'll treat him. He's acting like a baby, so they won't hurt him."

If that was Moon's strategy, it didn't work.

As if they were launched by a starting gun, the two herd stallions charged. Moon stopped.

"My gosh, listen to them." Jen gasped.

Eight galloping hooves sounded like thunder.

Moon's hesitant nicker asked a question, but no horse answered. Trying to hold his ground against the stallions' onslaught would be suicide, and finally Moon figured that out.

He wheeled away and ran. Quickly, he outdistanced the chestnut. But the Phantom was almost upon him. Father and son ran with heads level, legs reaching, and bellies low to the ground. The Phantom's white muzzle touched Moon's long black tail.

"Moon, get out of there!" Sam couldn't help calling out, though the young stallion obeyed an instinct stronger than any human voice.

He'd run away to survive, but Moon was still determined to have a herd. If he couldn't join one, he'd try to steal one. And so, black legs slanting, he veered right and raced back toward Yellowtail.

Surprised at Moon's return, the chestnut watched him flash by. But when Moon angled toward his grazing mares, Yellowtail screamed. He lunged after the black and punished him with a savage bite.

Defeated for now, Moon ran north. As Sam and Jen watched, he splashed across the river.

The Phantom turned back to his mares, who seemed more interested in grazing than greeting their protector. He urged them away from the river, up the hill, and along a series of switchbacks to safety.

Hooves hit places where shadows had kept ice from melting. It sounded as if the horses were tramping through snow cones.

Yellowtail waited until the Phantom's herd had vanished. At last, he darted down to La Charla for water. His head dipped three times before he let the mares take his place. Then, while their muzzles were still dripping, he herded them away.

When Ace and Popcorn neighed after the wild ones, Sam felt strangely weak.

"And *that*," Jen said with a sigh, "is why my mother is absolutely insane to want to move to the city."

Sam found herself nodding . . . until Jen's words sank in.

"Your mom wants to move?" She gasped. It was hard to believe that Lila Kenworthy, a former rodeo queen and fourth-generation rancher, would consider leaving the range. "Are you serious?"

Jen moved her hand as if shooing a mosquito. "Can we please not talk about it?"

"Yeah," Sam agreed, but she knew she wouldn't forget. Jen was her best friend. "But if there's anything I can do to help—"

"I'll not only let you know, I'll *make* you do it," Jen insisted with a weak smile.

For a few minutes, Jen and Sam let their horses meander toward the cattle. Over and over, Ace and Popcorn snorted, flared their nostrils, and breathed the scents of the free mustangs.

"You know," Sam said, "instead of riding over to Deerpath Ranch to visit Mrs. Allen, I'd like to check on Moon."

"That was a bad bite," Jen said, nodding.

"We have to cross back over the river, then go up the ridge." Sam hesitated for a second. Then she told herself to stop being a sissy.

Most people lived in cougar country their whole lives and never saw one. Besides, it was still daylight. There was little chance the cougar would be out hunting.

"I am getting sort of cold, too," Jen said. In turn, she raised her hands and blew on her knuckles.

"You'll warm right up in the canyon," Sam said, "because of the drop in altitude."

"Let's go," Jen said.

They reined their horses around, crossed back over the bridge at River Bend, then headed for Aspen Creek.

❊ ❊ ❊

"Are you sure we're going the right way?" Jen asked about twenty-five minutes later.

"I'm sure," Sam said.

"The footing is awful and the horses hate it."

Jen was right. It hadn't felt warm today, but snow was melting and the mud was thick. In some places, the horses' hooves made sucking sounds. In other places, snow looked like frosting on the top of branches, but it dripped down on the girls' hair.

"This is not warming me up, Samantha," Jen said after a splat of slush landed on her shoulder.

"We're almost there," Sam promised. "See up there? I remember that kind of curled-over snowbank."

"Popcorn is going nuts," Jen muttered. "His skin's twitching and—"

"His eyes are rolling," Sam finished.

Ace tensed below her. Then he stopped and refused to go on.

If he heard the same sound she did, he shouldn't worry. It was probably just more snow dripping. But all at once, Sam knew she was wrong.

About ten feet ahead, just off the trail, a cougar crouched and lapped at the snow.

Topaz. The word popped into Sam's mind because the young cougar was exactly that golden-brown color. The tip of his tail twitched as he watched the riders, but he wasn't about to leave his find.

"Jen." Sam barely breathed the name.

"I see it."

The young cougar was eating a deer half buried in the snow. A patch of grass showed green near the dead deer. Could the crest of snow overhead have avalanched down as it grazed?

Sam almost had the scene figured out when Popcorn bolted. Jen's reins were tight, wrapped around her fists, but the albino seemed determined to go over backward rather than stay near the cat.

Sam couldn't take her eyes from the eating cougar, but she motioned with her head for Jen to let Popcorn go farther along the ridge, back toward River Bend.

"Come on," Jen whispered. "You have to come with me."

Sam shook her head and still didn't look away.

Ace was restless and worried. He wanted to follow Popcorn, but he wasn't panicked. Sam knew he'd stay, so she held up one finger, signaling she'd be there in a minute. She didn't check Jen's expression and it was probably just as well. Jen would think she was being foolhardy.

The cat left off eating to watch Popcorn go. His tail lashed in irritation. As he chewed each mouthful, he raised amber eyes to watch Sam.

What had Dad said? Cougars needed a deer a week to survive. If that was true, and the young cat could keep his cache safe from coyotes, he ought to be set for a while.

Hooves splattered in the mud behind Sam.

Popcorn had been in such a frenzy, Sam couldn't believe Jen would ride back. Behind her, Sam heard a snort.

Ace returned it and stamped a front hoof. Ahead of her, the cougar stopped eating.

There was another snort then, but it sounded lower, hoarser than Popcorn's, and Sam allowed her head to turn just a fraction of an inch.

Moon stood about three yards from Ace. He tilted his head and trotted toward the cougar.

Chapter Thirteen

Hissing and snarling, the cougar backed away from the horses and, reluctantly, from its food.

Ace wanted to escape the fierce, threatening sounds. Sam tensed her legs, hands, and seat, trying to keep the gelding from backing down the steep trail that descended from the ridge. It was no use. No matter what she did, Ace refused to stay near the cougar. Partly because Sam believed Ace's instincts were better than hers, she finally let him put some distance between them and the furious cat.

At last, he stopped. Though Ace continued to shift, Sam was able to look back at the two wild animals. Moon hadn't advanced a step nearer the cougar. He was being careful, but he shook his head, scattering his forelock away from his eyes.

Was it a threat?

Whatever Moon meant, the cougar didn't like it. He leaped for the icy shelf above the deer. Though the shelf was twice as high as the roof of a car, the cat made it with ease.

Suddenly, Sam could imagine what had happened. The cougar had poised on the snowy ledge, ready to pounce on the grazing deer. Then, just as the cat pushed off for its attack, the shelf had broken and caused a small avalanche of snow that had killed the deer.

Now, white fangs gleaming, the cougar growled at Moon. When a chunk of snow fell, Moon jumped back. The move opened the bite on his haunch and fresh bleeding began.

As soon as the stallion turned back the way he'd come and trotted away, the cougar leaped down. He stood next to his meal, but his eyes followed Moon.

Though the horse had vanished, the cougar lifted his head, and Sam felt chills. Was he smelling the blood on the wind?

For a minute, she had wondered if the two lonely animals could share Aspen Creek canyon in peace.

That had been a childish hope. Predator and prey might be fascinated by one another, but they could never be friends.

Sam looked down the hillside and saw Jen and Popcorn waiting for her. When she reached them, Sam expected Jen to give her an angry lecture. She didn't. She stayed quiet, even when Sam broke the silence.

"We stayed back far enough that Ace could've

gotten us away," Sam said.

Jen shrugged as if she didn't care, and Sam kicked herself. Jen was already upset over her parents' problems and the prospect of moving; Sam needed to cheer her up. Instead, she'd given her more to worry about.

"We'd better hurry. The sun's starting to set," Sam said.

Jen nodded, and urged Popcorn into a jog. Ace matched the albino's pace, and the girls slowed the horses only when River Bend Ranch was in sight.

Gram was standing on the front porch watching the ridge when Sam and Jen rode into the yard.

"Looks like trouble," Sam said under her breath.

Jen flashed her a look that said Sam would have to handle any explanations.

"You didn't go over to Trudy Allen's," Gram said. "I called and asked her if I could borrow an egg for my cake, since the hens are edgy and laying poorly. Then, not ten minutes ago, she called back and asked if you were still coming by."

"I'm sorry, Gram," Sam apologized. "We were watching some wild horses and it got late, so we didn't go."

"That doesn't explain why Jennifer is pale as milk."

Jen's hand flew up to rub her cheek, as if she could work some color into her face.

Sam opened her mouth to answer Gram's comment, but nothing came out.

"Never mind," Gram said. "I'd best get Jen home. Meanwhile, Samantha, you cool down both those horses. Take your time and don't let them stiffen up."

"Gram!" Sam's voice soared with indignation. How could Gram think she'd neglect the horses?

Gram had already ducked back inside for her car keys. When she bustled back out, she kept giving orders.

"And there's no reason you can't start dinner," she said. "Your father's eating at Brynna's, so you and I will just have soup and sandwiches."

As Gram and Jen drove away, Blaze trotted across the ranch yard to stand beside Sam.

"What is this, Blaze?" she asked. The Border collie looked up at her. "I have to take care of both horses and make dinner. Is this punishment or does Gram just want my help?"

The little brown dots of fur over Blaze's eyes shifted up and down. Once he decided all her talking wasn't an offer of dog chow, Blaze trotted back to the house, threw himself down on a step and went to sleep.

It took Sam forever to walk both horses and brush them. Still scared, Popcorn longed to be back in the corral with his adopted herd. He was so skittish, Ace almost nipped him.

"You're getting quite the little attitude, aren't you, boy?" Sam said to Ace after she'd turned Popcorn out. "But I'll take the blame. I shouldn't have made you stay near that cougar. It's against all your instincts and you did it just for me."

Sam rubbed the white star on Ace's forehead. She would have kissed his nose, too, but the gelding started pulling toward the barn.

"Are you telling me I can repay your loyalty with a little grain?" Sam let the gelding tow her along to the barn. She spent extra time rubbing Ace down, too, but Gram still wasn't back by the time she finished.

Sam returned to the house. Blaze squeezed through the door beside her, followed her to the walk-in pantry, and sat down where he could watch.

"There's no dog food in here," she warned, but Blaze's tail thumped the floor anyway.

Sam considered the canned soup. Gram hadn't said which kind she wanted.

"Tomato. Chicken noodle. Clam chowder. Cream of mushroom." Sam read the labels to Blaze and his tail thumped some more.

In spite of the dog's appreciation, Sam didn't know which to choose. Then she looked at a shelf stacked with about a dozen cans of tuna.

Got it, Sam thought.

"Tuna salad sandwiches and clam chowder go together, right?" Sam left the pantry with a can in each hand and Blaze dancing beside her. "They're both seafood."

The phone began ringing before she'd opened either can.

"Hello?" Sam said, expecting it to be Gram.

It was Brynna. "Sam, your dad said I didn't need to call, but I had to. Nothing's wrong," Brynna hurried on, "I just wanted to know if you've seen either of our juvenile delinquents lately."

Sam hesitated. Of course, Brynna meant Moon and the cougar. Sam wanted to tell her everything, but how would Dad react to Brynna's side of the conversation?

Dad had said he'd give the cougar a chance. Two or three days, he'd said, if no River Bend stock was hurt. Which it hadn't been. The cougar hadn't come near the house, either. That spot on the ridge was several miles away.

"I saw them both today," Sam said.

"Where?" Brynna asked.

"The Phantom had his herd just across the river, and Moon tried to join up."

"I can't say he's a fast learner," Brynna said. Then she spoke an aside to Dad, mumbling "Moon" and, "I'll tell you later."

"He interrupted a fight, though. There's a chestnut herd stallion who used to be part of Moon's bachelor band. He and the Phantom were discussing who had grazing rights when Moon came loping in. Then they ganged up on him."

"I don't know what the Phantom is thinking," Brynna said. "This sparring is a spring and summer game. Once feed gets scarce, he's not going to have the energy to do all this fighting."

"I've been wondering about that, too," Sam admitted. "But when he left today, he looked like he was headed back the way he usually comes in for water."

"Good," Brynna said. "At least he's out of that disputed area in Lost Canyon. It looks like half of Arroyo Azul is tribal land, but I'll tell you about that later."

"Are you talking to me or my dad?" Sam asked.

"Definitely you." Brynna sounded amused. "Wyatt left the kitchen when I said I didn't know what the Phantom was thinking."

Sam laughed. Dad cared for every animal on River Bend and for wild animals, too, but he had no patience with anyone who attributed human qualities to them.

"And the cougar?" Brynna's voice sobered. "Wyatt said he was down by your chicken coop."

"He's up on the ridge now, about midway between River Bend and Three Ponies," Sam said.

"Tell me everything," Brynna insisted.

Sam did, including her theory about how the deer had died.

"We can't assume he's hunting, then," Brynna said. "I'm going to contact someone in the Department of Wildlife, just in case."

"What happens then?" Sam asked.

"They can relocate nuisance animals."

"Is he really a nuisance?"

"Not yet." Brynna sighed. "But we need a plan in case he becomes one."

"I'm afraid hanging around the ranches looking for food is so much easier than hunting . . ."

"Right," Brynna said. "But I'll get on the phone tomorrow. Maybe in the meantime, instinct will tell him he's better off in the mountains."

Sam felt a little better. The cougar had watched his mother for at least a year, and he had inborn instincts he couldn't ignore. He might be all right, after all.

"Okay, Sam," Brynna said. "Your dad's making starving noises. I've got to go take a pizza out of the oven."

"You can make pizza?" Sam asked.

"Sure, if it's take-and-bake from the deli in Darton," Brynna said, laughing.

"That sounds good to me," Sam said, considering the two unopened cans on the kitchen counter.

"Well, it's lucky Wyatt's not marrying me for my domestic skills. I've been living on salads and noodles for years. I can't remember the last time I made a meal that required more than one cooking utensil."

Sam felt a little envious. Cooking whatever you wanted, whenever you liked, sounded independent and altogether fun.

She glanced at the kitchen window. It was dark. She couldn't have more than a few minutes before Gram returned.

"Ouch!" Brynna yelped, and Sam heard the slam of an oven door. "So, if your Gram mentions retiring, you'd better stock up on vitamins. Gotta go," she said quickly.

"'Bye—and let me know what the wildlife people say, okay?"

"You bet," Brynna answered.

As soon as Sam hung up the phone, she attacked the cans with Gram's creaky hand-held can opener. Sam preferred the electric one that Gram had stashed in some bottom cupboard, but she didn't have time to find it.

She glanced at the clock again, and then at the darkness pressing against the kitchen windows, and resisted a pinch of worry.

Sam almost hoped Gram got home and found her slacking, because she had been gone almost two hours for a half-hour trip.

Chapter Fourteen

*A*s wind chased around the ranch house, Sam told herself the weather wasn't bad enough to delay Gram. More likely, something was going on at the Kenworthys' place.

Sam tried to distract herself by considering her soup and sandwiches. Now she understood Gram's frustration when she finished preparing a meal and no one showed up to eat it.

Come and get it or I'll feed it to the dog, she'd heard Gram say more than once.

"You'd like that fine, wouldn't you, Blaze?" Sam asked, then moved to fill his food dish.

As she did, she heard Gram's Buick pull in.

Sam ladled soup into the bowls. She'd just placed them on the table when Gram came through the door and shut it against a cold gust of wind.

"I'm sorry to be late." Gram slipped off her coat, noticed the neatly set table, and smiled. "I tried to call."

"I was probably talking to Brynna," Sam said as Gram sat down. "She wanted to ask me about the cougar." Sam ate a bite of sandwich, wishing Gram would explain why she'd been gone so long. "They're having pizza."

"Well, I think this is a fine dinner. Did you use a touch of dill in the tuna salad?"

"No, nothing special," Sam said. She spooned up some soup, swallowed it, then lost her patience. "Was something wrong at Jen's house?"

"Not at all, honey. We were looking at the dress patterns Brynna and Helen Coley decided on for the wedding—for your dress and Brynna's. They're beautiful, and tomorrow after school Helen's going to pick you up, along with Jen and Rachel—"

"That's always fun," Sam muttered, but Gram pretended not to hear.

" —and start pinning the dress on you."

"What does it look like?"

"It's long." Gram's fingers moved across her collarbone, as if sketching the gown's neckline. "And it's got—" she broke off, then gave up. "Really, you should see the picture for yourself. I'm no good at fashion talk. But the fabric rustles and it's a dark Christmas tree green that will be beautiful with your auburn hair."

Sam smiled, then she thought of her homework. "Do you know how much I dislike algebra?" She groaned.

"I know your grade has improved. And I admire your hard work so much, I'll do these dishes so that you can get started on your studies."

"Okay," Sam said, but before she could zip open her backpack, the telephone rang.

Gram answered it, then held her hand over the mouthpiece. "If I'm not mistaken, it's the Slocum girl."

"Rachel?" Sam asked. What could she want?

The only other time Rachel had called had been on the afternoon of Linc Slocum's big Brahma-Que. Then, she had asked Sam and Jake to pick up a bag of ice.

As she took the phone from Gram, Sam thought the chances were good Rachel hadn't called just to chat.

Sam was right. Rachel didn't pretend it was a social call. She didn't even say hello.

"You've got to decide," she insisted as soon as Sam picked up the phone. "Should I buy Mocha?"

"Rachel, I don't know," Sam began.

"You have to decide now. Tonight."

"No, I don't," Sam said, but curiosity ran neck-in-neck with her irritation. "What's the emergency?"

"Katie Sterling called from Sterling Stables and said they'd had another offer on Mocha, but she was giving me first right of refusal, whatever that means."

"It sounds like, since you showed interest in the mare first, they're giving you a chance to beat what-ever this other person has offered to pay for her,"

Sam said. "Have you asked your dad?"

"My dad doesn't care what I decide," Rachel said. "It's Ryan."

"Your twin?"

"Yes. He knows about horses, and he'll think I'm smart or stupid depending on—" As if she was embarrassed by her own honesty, Rachel broke off. "I've told you all this before. Just decide."

"Rachel, I can't. You haven't ridden Mocha or handled her. All we know is that she's pretty. She might buck. She might bite. She might be barn sour."

There was a moment of quiet from the other end of the line. Sam looked up to see Gram scrubbing the soup pot with a half smile on her lips.

"Barn sour," Rachel repeated. "Is that a breath problem?"

"No. Lots worse," Sam said, shaking her head. "It means you get on her and ride her for a few minutes, and when she decides she's had enough, she goes home. Whether you want to or not."

"She thinks for herself, you mean," Rachel said. "What's wrong with that?"

"Rachel, she's not a person. She's a horse, and she's trained, or should be, to work *with* you." Sam sighed, feeling sorry for any horse that became Rachel's. "And one *really* bad idea," she warned, "is to take a smart, spirited horse and just lock her up. Are you willing to exercise her?"

"You're just being mean about this," Rachel said,

"when you should be flattered."

"I was flattered, at first," Sam admitted. "But I'd have to be pretty silly to keep feeling flattered when you won't listen to my suggestions."

"Well, I don't want to ride her in front of people."

That must mean Rachel had been listening. Sam softened, trying one last time to help.

"Rachel, why don't you just tell Katie Sterling you are interested. Then, your dad would trust Jed Kenworthy's opinion, so maybe —"

"He doesn't need an expert opinion. He needs to know I *want* that horse. I'm the only one who cares if she's worth buying."

"Fine. Then why don't you have Jed go over and check Mocha out tomorrow?"

"Because"— Rachel's voice rose in a sort of trill, and Sam wondered how a single word could imply the listener was stupid — "tomorrow, Jed's driving my dad to the airport so he can fly to New York. Some people yearn for civilization, if you know what I mean?" Rachel chuckled. "But then, you probably don't."

Sam's feelings might have been hurt if she hadn't been so irritated. But she was. *Really* irritated.

"Rachel, I've got an idea," Sam said. "Why don't you do whatever you want and so will I? Right now, though I can hardly believe it, I want to go do my algebra homework. See you at school."

It took all Sam's self-control not to slam down the

receiver. She replaced it gently and stood with her hand on it, as if it might pop back up, with Rachel still chattering.

"I won't even ask what Rachel wanted," Gram said, "but it sounded as if you did a fine job of staying polite."

"She thinks she's a *queen*," Sam fumed. "And if you don't hop to obey her commands, you're, you're —" She searched for a word. "You're *nothing*. Sure, I was polite, but what does that accomplish?"

Gram rinsed two spoons before she answered.

"I know it's tempting to give Rachel a taste of her own medicine, but there's something you should remember: bad deeds have a nasty way of coming home to roost." Gram tilted her head as she met Sam's eyes. "So do good deeds. You just have to decide which ones you want returning."

High winds blew in overnight. On Thursday morning, they seemed to have swept away Jen's low spirits.

Sam and Jen shivered and talked at the bus stop. They considered the white skies and hoped for sledding during winter break.

Once they were at school and headed for their lockers, Jen asked, "How did you do with those polynomials? I called to see if you needed help, but your line was busy forever. What were you doing, talking to Rachel?" Jen gave a self-mocking smile.

Sam wasn't sure how to explain. Jen was pretty sensitive on this subject.

"Well, actually . . ." Sam began.

Jen struck her forehead with one mittened hand.

"No, wait," Sam said, then nodded down the hall.

Rachel clicked in their direction. She wore high-heeled boots, a sleek fudge-brown skirt, and a matching blouse that shimmered just a shade lighter. Her head was bent to hear the latest gossip from Daisy. Other girls, dressed more for nightlife than a snowy school day, tagged along. They looked as if they were hoping for crumbs of Her Majesty's attention.

"Really, Jen, you'll like this." Sam held Jen's arm to keep her from veering off, then waited until Rachel was about a yard away. "Hi, Rachel, thanks for calling last night."

The girls around Rachel stopped, shocked. Rachel kept walking, though an attractive little frown marked her brow as she gazed over Sam's head.

"Daisy, did you hear something like the squeak of a very, very small insect?" Rachel asked.

"I didn't hear a thing," Daisy chirped, tossing her long blond hair. "But I see a most amazing sweater."

The other girls giggled, nudging each other as they gaped at Jen's harvest fair sweater. Although Sam didn't appreciate the gold-and-pumpkin plaid as much as Jen obviously did, she figured her friend should be able to wear whatever she wanted without criticism.

"She must be wearing it on a dare. There's no other

possible explanation," Rachel said. Then she and her entourage moved on in a cloud of mingled perfume.

Sam tried to let the comment pass. She tried to remember how Gram had cautioned her against bad deeds. But she couldn't let Rachel get away with insulting Jen like that.

"Hey, Rachel," Sam said, and Rachel glared back over her shoulder, eyebrows raised. "I hope you don't pay someone to come up with your snotty remarks, because if do, you're getting robbed."

The girls twittered on down the hall. The farther they got, the more confused Sam felt. Why had Jen, who always had a comeback, kept quiet?

"Does that answer your question about what great friends I am with Rachel?" Sam asked Jen.

"Oh, yeah. And it was lots of fun," Jen said, but her expression seemed to ask if Sam knew what she'd gotten herself into.

"Why are you giving me that look?" Sam demanded.

"Well, I can't help wondering how much *more* fun it's going to be after school."

Now it was Sam's turn to hit her brow in dismay. Jen gave Sam a one-armed hug, then a gentle push toward history. As she walked, Sam tried to figure a way out of riding home in the same car as Rachel.

Maybe there'd be a blizzard and they'd all have to stay at school. If so, she'd make sure to slip out of journalism, so she wouldn't be trapped with Rachel.

Maybe there'd be a flood and all of Darton High

would be evacuated to a Red Cross shelter in Sacramento. If so, she'd offer to clean out lavatories, rather than stay near Rachel.

Maybe there'd be an invasion of space aliens. . . .

Almost anything sounded better than reality. She couldn't stand the thought of being confined in the backseat of the Slocums' Mercedes when Mrs. Coley picked them up to drive Jen, Sam, and Rachel to the Gold Dust Ranch today.

After school, Sam and Jen stood waiting. Gulls spun in a flock above the Darton High parking lot, but Mrs. Coley was nowhere in sight.

"People always say that means a storm at sea," Jen mused as she looked at the gulls. "But that's a long flight to come to a place as cold as this. I think I'd stay at the beach and wait out the rain."

"They're just cruising over the parking lot for the leftover lunches," Sam said. "Or the remains of students who've been stared to death by Rachel."

"I bet she's not looking forward to this forced neighborliness any more than we are," Jen said.

Sam had to agree. "There's Mrs. Coley." She pointed as the blue Mercedes-Benz rolled among the student cars.

"Let's go," Jen said.

They bolted toward the car. Once there, they greeted Mrs. Coley, slid into the backseat, and fastened their seat belts.

When Rachel arrived, she didn't say a word. She

sat in the front seat and waited for Mrs. Coley to take her home.

On the way to the Gold Dust Ranch, Mrs. Coley entertained Sam and Jen with descriptions of the dress Brynna had picked out for Sam to wear as maid of honor.

Apparently, the pattern for the dress was a tricky one. Mrs. Coley joked about how long it had taken her to make even a "rough draft" of the dress. Rachel sat like a statue, ignoring the whole conversation.

Sam had only been to the Gold Dust Ranch three times since the Slocums had moved in, and the last time she hadn't really noticed the grand entrance to the ranch because she'd been worried about Rachel. Linc Slocum had declared her missing, and Sam and Jake joined the search party—but Rachel, of course, had been fine.

Now, Sam was impressed all over again by the soaring iron gate, which swung open at the touch of a remote control button inside the Mercedes.

The car rolled along a paved road, past flower beds planted with some kind of bright bush that had survived the cold. Farther on, white wooden fences lined pastures filled with healthy livestock.

On the right, Sam saw Danish Belted and blue-black Angus cattle. Next came a fenced field that held a dozen Brahmas, including the brindle bull named Maniac.

On the left, a herd of Shetland ponies roamed a rolling pasture. One ran along the fence, and his shaggy charcoal mane looked as full as a lion's.

The Shetlands were so cute and fuzzy, Sam wanted to give one a hug. In the next minute she felt a stab of worry. The ponies wouldn't be much of a match for even an inexperienced cougar.

Up ahead stood the foreman's house. The log cabin had been the Kenworthys' when the ranch was still the Lazy K, before hard times forced them to sell out to Linc Slocum. Sam thought it looked cozy and perfect for the high desert setting.

Mrs. Coley paused to let Sam and Jen out.

"I'll be back in a few minutes, girls," Mrs. Coley said. "As soon as I drop off Rachel."

At that, Rachel gave a little flounce of temper, but still didn't speak.

Sam watched the car continue past redwood hitching posts with brass rings, straight ahead to the hump that had been bulldozed from the surrounding land so that the Slocums' home could be built on a man-made hilltop.

Even though Jen saw the white-pillared mansion every day, she stared, too.

"I never stop wondering why they thought it would be a good idea to build a replica of a Southern mansion in the middle of cowboy country." Jen started up the path to her own one-story cabin. "Could a building be more misplaced?"

Sam gave the mansion one more look. She wondered which wing held Rachel's bedroom suite with hot tub and entertainment center, but she didn't ask

Jen. Sam was pretty sure her friend had never been invited inside.

"I think that place is perfect for Linc and Rachel," said Sam as she followed Jen. Gram would be proud, Sam thought, that she hadn't said that the mansion looked stiff and show-offy, just like the people who lived there.

"We'll see if Ryan likes it," Jen said. "I don't think he's ever been here."

"But you have high hopes, don't you?" Sam asked as Jen opened the door to her house.

"I really do," Jen admitted. "Sometimes, I can be quite optimistic."

Inside Jen's house, a fire crackled in the fireplace and the scent of cinnamon mixed with wood smoke. Sam felt immediately at home.

"Hello, Samantha," Lila Kenworthy said as she came slowly from the kitchen. "How was your day, Jen?"

"Fine, Mom."

"Why don't you all come into the kitchen?" Lila had a faint Texas accent and short blond hair. Her blue eyes looked weary. "We'll have a snack while we wait for Helen."

Maybe Lila was just tired, Sam thought as she drank the milky tea and ate the honey-spice cookies Jen's mother set before them.

"Mrs. Coley does a lot of sewing at our house because she only has one room up there," Jen explained, nodding toward the Slocums' mansion. "And the light in our living room is good most of the day."

"I bet it's because the company's better," Sam said, and felt pleased that Lila smiled. She couldn't really be thinking of moving, could she?

"Brynna won't be by until tonight," Lila told Sam. "I guess you knew that?"

"No, but it doesn't matter. I've been seeing her plenty these days."

Lila and Jen met each others' eyes.

"Things are going great," Sam hurried to assure them. "I think we'll be fine."

"All families have their problems," Lila said. "But Brynna and Wyatt seem real happy whenever I see them together."

When Mrs. Coley arrived, she showed Sam a copy of *Bride's* magazine and pointed to the dress Brynna wanted Sam to wear.

The floor-length gown had spaghetti straps and a snug bodice that narrowed down to a tight waist, then flowed into full skirts that would rustle when she walked.

"And because it's winter, I'll be making some kind of a little jacket to go over it. Lace probably," Mrs. Coley said, tapping another picture. "And here's the material." Mrs. Coley took a swath of shiny material from a pink paper bag.

"It's great," Sam said. She could picture herself moving down a church aisle with formal grace, and she couldn't help wishing there'd be someone watching and appreciating her.

Dad will, she thought suddenly.

He might be marrying Brynna, but it would be the first time he'd see his daughter in a formal gown. If it looked anything like the photograph, Sam thought she'd look pretty enough to make him proud.

"Today, I'd like to get started pinning it on you," Mrs. Coley said.

"Okay," Sam said softly, wondering why this dress felt so important.

She stood with her arms out. Because Gram had sewn a lot of her clothes when she was little, Sam knew how to stand still while a tissue paper pattern of the dress was slipped over her head, then pulled and pinned into place.

Before Mrs. Coley was done pinning, Sam heard the rumbling of a truck outside. Tires crunched, gears made grinding sounds, and Sam heard lots of high-pitched neighs.

Jen's pale eyebrows arched above the frames of her glasses as Lila went to the window and pulled back the curtain to peer out.

Sam barely understood the words Mrs. Coley uttered through the straight pins clamped in her lips, but it sounded like, "What's all the ruckus?"

"It's a big horse van from"—Lila paused, then read—"Sterling Stables."

Sam gasped. *Rachel had done it. She'd bought Mocha.*

"I don't remember"—Mrs. Coley took the pins from her mouth and set them aside—"that we're expecting any pickups or deliveries, do you, Lila?"

Mrs. Coley lifted the pattern off, and Sam ducked her head to avoid the pricking pins.

"No. Definitely not." Lila's hands perched on her hips. "Jed would never schedule the arrival of a new horse when he was gone."

"Rachel would," Sam said.

Lila, Mrs. Coley, and Jen all turned to stare at her, in spite of the commotion outside.

"Whatever would Rachel want with a horse?" Mrs. Coley asked.

"She's been thinking about getting a Morgan mare named Mocha," Sam answered.

"Hasn't she given up the idea of being a rodeo queen?" Lila turned to Jen.

"How would I know?" Jen snapped. "Rachel sure doesn't share her secrets with me. If Sam says Rachel wants a Morgan mare—"

Before Jen finished, the cabin door flew open so hard, it hit the wall and nearly bounced closed in Rachel's flushed and frantic face.

She was still dressed in her high-fashion clothes, but her hair wasn't sleek, and she was wobbling a little. It looked as if she'd broken the heel off one of her knee-high boots.

"You've got to help me." Rachel gasped. "One of you who"—her hands fluttered wildly—"does horses. They got Mocha into the pen all right, but all those little ponies escaped into the mountains."

Chapter Fifteen

$\mathcal{S}$am and Jen slipped past Rachel through the door and stared around the ranch yard.

Rachel couldn't possibly have lost an entire herd of ponies, could she?

A brown Morgan mare trotted up and down the front fence of the pasture that had held the ponies. It was Mocha, and she was all alone.

Mrs. Coley, Lila, Jen, and Rachel were all outside now.

"Did your father know this mare was on her way?" Lila rubbed her brow in confusion.

"No. I ordered her and I paid for her. Katie Sterling had no qualms about billing Mocha to my credit card. There weren't *any* problems." Rachel took a long breath and added, "At first."

As soon as Rachel was quiet, everyone else began asking questions.

"Why didn't you put the new mare in the round pen?"

"How did the ponies get loose?"

"Where did the horse van go?"

Sam couldn't tell who was asking what. Apparently, neither could Rachel, because she put her hands over her ears, then shouted, "If my dad was here, you wouldn't be ganging up on me."

There was a moment's quiet. Then Rachel's hands fell away from her ears.

"We just want to know what happened so we can help." Mrs. Coley kept her tone level.

Rachel looked hopefully at Sam.

"I asked before, but I guess you didn't hear me. Why didn't you have them put Mocha in the round pen by herself?" Sam asked.

"That's what that driver said, too." Rachel's tone dismissed them both. "But Mocha is my horse, and I thought she would like being the only big horse among all those munchkins."

Rachel nodded as if she were an expert, but Sam decided Rachel's horse psychology told more about her than it did Mocha.

"Those munchkins," Jen said, "are registered Shetland ponies bred and raised in the Shetland Islands."

"So they're hardy," Mrs. Coley mused. "That's good. If this snowstorm breaks, they should be able to withstand it."

"They're tougher, stockier, and have heavier coats than American Shetland ponies," Jen conceded, "but they're also smaller."

Involuntarily, Sam looked toward the ridge.

"You're worried about that orphaned cougar, aren't you, Samantha?" Lila's voice lowered to a whisper. "That was a sorry idea from the first."

Jen's expression flickered between anger and sympathy, then she squared her shoulders.

"Look, I don't think the ponies went far," Jen said. "They're all tubby little guys. They like their feed. As soon as they hear me filling that manger with grain, I bet they'll come trotting back home."

Without waiting for a second opinion, Jen headed for the barn.

"How, exactly, did this happen?" Mrs. Coley asked.

"Just the way I said!" Rachel insisted.

"I admit I'm surprised," Lila said. "I'd heard such good things about Sterling Stables . . ."

Sam watched Rachel squirm as Lila continued.

". . . and for that driver to just create this mess, then leave, is not reputable behavior."

"How did the ponies escape?" Sam asked.

"The driver agreed to do what I told him, and he asked me to hold the gate open while he unloaded Mocha. And then—" Rachel shuddered. "All those furry ponies started crowding against the gate. And one of them started rubbing its little whiskery chin against my hand, and then it nipped me!"

Rachel snatched both hands against her chest as if the terrible event had just happened again.

"So you jumped back and they all got out," Sam said.

"The driver wanted to help catch them," Rachel said, "but I couldn't let him."

"Couldn't?" Mrs. Coley echoed.

Rachel lifted her nose an inch toward the sky.

"You don't know how it is. People in our position are always targets for gossip. If I'd let that man stay, he would be telling everyone he came into contact with about my 'mistake.'"

As Rachel finished, Sam turned to Lila and Mrs. Coley. Both women looked as if they were deciding whether they should lecture Rachel or laugh at her. Everyone except Rachel could see she was responsible for this disaster.

Suddenly, Sam thought she heard raindrops. Next, she saw Jen shaking a big silver grain scoop, and the pattering sound grew louder.

Five ponies, all in shades of brown, rounded the corner of the Brahma corral at a run.

"Here they come!" Lila cheered. "Good work, honey."

Mrs. Coley hurried ahead of Jen. She flashed her arm back and forth, making Mocha shy away. Then she opened the gate so that Jen could lead the crowding, pushing ponies through.

"How many were there?" Sam asked Rachel.

"How should I know?" Rachel laughed, amazed Sam would ask her.

Frustrated, Sam looked at Jen's mother for an answer.

"Seven, I think," Lila said. "The one piebald and the tiniest gelding aren't with this bunch."

"Is the tiniest one a gray with a bushy mane and tail?" Sam asked.

"That sounds more like a squirrel—" Rachel began, but Lila spoke right over her.

"That's the one," Lila said. "He's a scamp. I bet he hightailed off somewhere and only the piebald was foolish enough to go with him."

The slam of the pasture gate made Sam turn in time to see Mocha trot up to cautiously touch noses with the ponies. As soon as she'd bolted the gate, Jen hurried back toward Sam.

"Two are still missing. If we saddle up right now, we could find them before sundown."

"Great," Rachel urged. "You do that."

"May I borrow a horse?" Sam asked.

"Sure, yeah. Take any horse you want," Rachel said.

"Wait a minute." Lila's arms were crossed hard and her lips made a straight line.

Sam knew Lila didn't want them riding out while the cougar was roaming nearby.

"Mom, I know what you're thinking, but there's no way in the world I'd risk Silly by getting too close to a cougar." Jen took a deep breath, then expelled it. "Even if it was stalking the ponies."

Lila gave a slight nod, believing her daughter.

"As long as you bring them back safely," Rachel added.

Sam watched Rachel's fingers flutter through her hair again and again. Was Rachel so spoiled that she didn't realize her mistake might put others, especially the ponies, in danger?

As they hurried toward the barn, Sam thought of the mare she'd borrowed on the day Rachel "disappeared." The mare had been surefooted and steady, even when the Phantom appeared.

"I don't remember her name, but there's a pinto mare with a scarred knee," Sam began.

"Patches. She'd be good." Jen answered automatically, but her eyes were fixed on the ground and she chewed at her bottom lip. "I'm deciding whether to take Silly, after all."

Sam had a sensible suggestion. Shouldn't they ride the horses that had faced the cougar and the gunfire that killed her, and then carried her body home?

This would be a bad time to make Jen mad, but Sam had to risk it. "Which horses did your dad and Linc ride? Before?"

Jen answered without hesitation, "Linc rode Champ and my dad took Sundance."

"Wow," Sam said, surprised. She wouldn't have guessed either horse would stay unruffled in such loud and unfamiliar circumstances.

"Yeah, the Kenworthy palominos came through," Jen said, sarcastically.

Jen was often sarcastic, but this time Sam couldn't figure it out. When Jen spoke again, Sam decided she must have been mistaken.

"So, I'll take Silly," Jen said. "Do you want to ride Champ?"

Sam tried to say no. She reminded herself how steady Patches had been. But then she thought of the palomino Quarter horse Linc Slocum rode with a severe bit and heavy hands. She'd love a chance to show Champ that not all riders were cruel.

Finally, she couldn't resist.

"Yes! I'd love to ride Champ! Let's go!"

The winter sky had turned gray by the time Champ and Silly were saddled. Trying to beat the invasion of dusk, Sam and Jen set out for the ridgeline at a lope.

Side by side, the two palominos surged up the path. They were always kept in the barn, blanketed, so they didn't have shaggy winter coats. Their muscles rolled under hides that shone like gold satin.

"They look and move alike, don't they?" Sam called to Jen.

Her friend nodded, but just as there'd been something sarcastic in Jen's tone when she talked about the Kenworthy palominos before, now her mouth twisted in a bitter smile.

Once, the Kenworthys' ranch had been famed for its palominos, but now only four remained. Sam guessed the horses were a reminder of better times.

When the horses reached the ridge top, the girls let them rest for a minute.

"Jen, if we see the ponies, do you think we can herd them back?"

"Yeah. I think they'll be hungry and ready to get back with their pals." Jen put Silly into a walk toward River Bend Ranch.

"I hope so," Sam said, glancing at her watch. "And I hope they're down this way, because it's almost sundown. If they've scampered off in some other direction, they're going to be roughing it tonight."

The girls rode along, eyes searching each clump of sagebrush, each stand of piñon pine. Except for a covey of startled quail, which ran twittering and flapping away from the horses, nothing moved.

"About five more minutes and we've got to turn around," Jen said. "You heard me promise Mom."

Sam nodded. At least the two ponies would have each other. Out in strange terrain, they'd be watchful and wary through the night.

Silly and Champ swung their heavy heads at the same time and looked down a ravine on their left.

Brush shook and then they saw that at least one of the ponies was safe.

The piebald pony wasn't trapped, but he was in a tight spot. His high-pitched whinny asked the big horses to wait.

"That's right, cutie," Jen crooned to the pony. "We're here to take you home."

"I wonder where the other one's gone?" Sam was glad they'd found this pony, but it meant the gray was out all alone.

"I don't know. But the cougar should still be eating that deer," Jen said. "And maybe the avalanche hit two of them. You can never tell."

The piebald pony made a halfhearted bolt up the side of the ravine.

"C'mon, you can make it," Jen called, but the pony shook his disheveled mane and stayed put.

"How do you want to do this?" Sam asked.

Her fingers touched the coiled rope held in a leather loop on Champ's saddle. The rope felt stiff and new, as if Linc only carried it for decoration.

"I'm a lousy roper, anyway," Sam said. "And this rope doesn't feel like it's been used much."

"I bet it hasn't." Jen tilted her head thoughtfully.

One white-blond braid swung away from her shoulder and swayed like a pendulum as she considered their situation as if it were a math problem.

"Okay," she said finally. "That pony knows me, but he has no idea who you are. So why don't you tie Champ, then climb down there, swinging the rope to spook Chipper. I'll pretend to ride away. Maybe he'll think he's being left behind with scary old you, and climb up here after us."

Sam nodded, but she didn't like Jen's solution. Steep downhills were her least favorite sort of riding, and she wasn't a lot more confident about doing them on foot. All she had to do was step on a loose rock and she'd go plunging headlong down the cliff.

"Okay, Champ," Sam said, unhooking the rope from the saddle. "Enjoy your rest. I'll go get the little guy."

The sidehill was sticky with mud, and Sam made it down without falling. It was surprisingly dark in the ravine, though it was only ten feet below the ridge trail.

Sam held an open loop in one hand and smooched to the pony as she swung the loop his way.

He stabbed at the hillside with hooves that would fit in teacups, and his small neigh made Sam feel like a bully.

"I'm doing this for your own good," she chirped. Then, as the piebald started up, she encouraged him. "Let's go! Upsy-daisy! C'mon!" Sam jogged up behind him and the pony bolted. "You've got it. Go!"

With a grunt, he reached the ridge, leaving Sam in the dark ravine.

"I'll keep him moving." Jen's voice floated back to Sam as she herded the pony toward home.

"Okay," Sam yelled, but the sides of the ravine absorbed the sound. She wasn't sure Jen had heard.

All at once, Sam shivered. She looked toward the darkest part of the ravine. Something rustled in the brush.

More quail, Sam decided. Just the same, she clambered back up the hill, stuck a muddy boot in

Champ's stirrup, and swung up.

"If it's all the same to you, let's get out of here," Sam said, touching her heels to the palomino's sides. He leaped after Silly and the piebald pony.

For an instant, Sam tried to look back at the bushes.

Night was falling fast, and the chasm below wouldn't reveal its secrets.

So, if a flash of fiery eyes seemed to show, deep in the ink-green bushes, it was probably just her imagination.

Chapter Sixteen

The piebald pony, with his large, irregular patches of black and white, was easy to follow through the dusk. He required no herding as he wended his way home. He moved at a trot where the trail was rough and rocked into a bound-for-home lope where the path was smooth.

Once the pony was back in the pasture, Sam and Jen faced the others.

"Good job, girls," Mrs. Coley called as she walked down the path from the mansion. Rachel followed a few haughty steps behind.

"Just in time, too." Lila rubbed her arms against the evening chill as she looked toward the road.

Sam knew Gram would arrive any minute to pick her up, but she didn't want to leave things unfinished.

"Jen," she said quietly, "do you think there's a chance your mom would let you skip school and go look for that pony in the morning?"

Apparently she hadn't been quiet enough, because Rachel made a mocking moan and rolled her eyes skyward. Even worse, Jen's mom had heard.

"Samantha Forster!" Lila Kenworthy sounded shocked.

Sam sucked in a breath. "I know it's not a great idea, and I never cut school, but what about that pony?"

Lila sighed and said, "I know he's not suited to spending a night on the range, but he'll live."

Looking through her fringe of wheat-colored hair, Lila Kenworthy appeared determined. Sam was glad when Jen took over negotiations.

"It's an emergency," Jen insisted. "Here's what we could do. Early tomorrow morning, before school, Sam leaves from River Bend, I leave from here, and we trap the pony between us."

Mrs. Coley looked half convinced, but Jen's mom wasn't.

"No," Lila said flatly. "There's a reason the hunting hours for cougars start a half hour before dawn."

Mrs. Coley shook her head, going over to Lila's side. "Girls, it's just too dangerous."

"Don't even worry about it," Rachel said, waving one hand. "There's no rush. My dad won't be home for days, and it's not like he'd notice one of them is missing."

Sam's anger boiled inside her. Rachel couldn't imagine the pony being attacked and killed. She only saw the inconvenience of going after him.

"When Jed comes back from the airport, I'll explain what's happened," Lila said. Her eyes slid toward Rachel.

Of course, she didn't take the hint. Rachel had put the pony in danger, but it didn't occur to her that she should confess.

At the sound of approaching tires, Sam turned. Gram was coming, and that gave her an idea.

"I'll tell my dad, too," Sam said, and suddenly her spirits lifted. "This is a slack time for the cowboys, and I bet they wouldn't mind looking for the pony."

As if to contradict Sam, a gust of icy wind sliced through the evening, making them shiver.

"Stand out here if you like," Rachel said, "but I'm going indoors where it's warm."

"What about your new horse?" Mrs. Coley asked quietly.

"Oh." Rachel stared at the dark chestnut mare who'd crowded against the white fence as if trying to escape the ponies. "What about her?"

"She was living in a stall at Sterling Stables," Sam said.

Rachel gave Jen an encouraging smile, as if she expected her to take over the chore of bedding down the mare. Jen pretended not to notice. She brushed imaginary dust from her hands, tugged at the cuffs of her sweater sleeves, then rubbed her palms together, warming them against the evening chill.

"I could lead her up to the barn, I guess." Rachel's

tone implied this was hardly her job.

"Good idea," Mrs. Coley said, then she turned briskly toward Sam. "You don't want to keep your grandmother waiting, honey."

Jen walked along beside Sam as she set out for Gram's car.

"If they don't find Chipper," Jen said, looking a little sheepish, "do you think Jake could track him?"

Jen and Jake did not have compatible personalities, but Sam knew her two best friends admired each other's skills.

Although Jen was a freshman, she was in Jake's physics class, and he grudgingly admitted her ability. Jen knew Jake's tracking skill was superb. The sheriff's department had even called on him to work with their adult experts while they tracked wild horse rustlers.

"Of course Jake would help." Sam gave Jen a hug, climbed into Gram's car, and turned the heater all the way up.

As soon as Sam saw her dad, she knew her predictions had been right. He was restless and frustrated by winter's inactivity.

When she and Gram came shivering into the kitchen, Dad stood in front of the stove, lifting lids and poking at stew with Gram's wooden spoon.

"I hate winter, and that's the truth," he greeted them.

Gram sighed as if she'd heard his complaint a hundred times. "Now, Wyatt, all spring, fall, and summer you complain about long hours and backaches. You pine for the winter so you'll be able to sit by the fire and read a book."

Wordless, Dad made room at the stove for Gram, then took a restless lap around the dining room table.

Finally, he shook his head in a self-mocking way.

"I know it. But I look at the clock, thinking this is about the time I should be riding in, rubbing down my horse before heading for the shower. Instead, I'm looking at the clock." Dad paused, and when he pointed at the clock, Sam noticed he was still holding Gram's spoon. "And I'm wondering what's on television and calculating how long I have to wait before I can decently go to bed."

"Go on out to the bunkhouse and harass your cowboys," Gram suggested. "And may I please have that spoon?" She took the wooden spoon back and tsked her tongue as if Dad were still a boy.

"I don't want to play cards and tell lies with the boys. I'm past that stage of my life."

Before Dad could think of phoning Brynna, Sam jumped in with a suggestion.

"Don't worry, Dad, I've got a real chore for you."

"Oh, you do?" Dad looked amused. "It wouldn't have to do with wild horses, would it?"

Sam hesitated. Did the mustangs need Dad's help?

Yesterday, the Phantom's herd had been pawing the frosty grass on the other side of La Charla. The silver stallion and his mares had looked fit and strong, though she didn't know where they were wintering.

And Moon? The young black stallion might be lonely, but he'd been born and bred on the range. She thought he was safe.

"No, Dad, it's not wild horses this time," Sam said. "It's a pony named Chipper. He belongs to the Slocums. He got out, and with this storm brewing . . ."

Sam didn't mention the cougar. She didn't have to.

"One of those fancy little imported ponies wouldn't stand a chance against that cat," Dad said, disgusted.

Sam felt a surge of protectiveness, but Dad stopped her before she could defend the pony.

"I'm not blaming the pony, Sam. I blame people. Some animals—people too—just don't transplant well. They need to be protected for their own good."

Sam saw a softening in Dad's expression and she knew he was thinking of her mother. Mom had been city-raised, but she'd fallen in love with wild Nevada.

"How did this pony get out?" he asked.

Gram finished spooning the dumplings on top of the stew, then turned to them with a humphing sound.

"Linc's out of town and his daughter charged a purebred Morgan mare—on her own credit card, I might add—to be delivered to the ranch." Gram held up a hand against Dad's astonishment. "In the excitement of the delivery, the entire bunch of ponies escaped. Your daughter helped bring back all but one of them."

"Gram? How did you know?" Sam was so amazed at Gram's recitation, she almost missed Dad's satisfied smile.

"Lila called while you and Jen were out chasing down the escapees," Gram said.

"How long till dinner?" Dad asked suddenly.

"Ten minutes, more or less," Gram said. "I'm just waiting for the dumplings to cook."

"I think I will walk out to the bunkhouse." Dad took his Stetson from a hook by the door and pulled it on with a contented nod. "I'll let the boys know we're going out at dawn and pen us a pony."

The Phantom called at midnight.

Half asleep, Sam sat up in bed, rubbing her eyes as her heart pounded. *Was it a dream?*

No. Hooves thundered on frozen ground, sounding so close she thought the stallion was in the ranch yard. He wouldn't be, though. The Phantom never crossed La Charla.

Downstairs, Blaze gave a gentle woof. Sam slid out of bed. The wooden floor sent chills through her toes and up her shins, but she stepped to the window.

A tracery of ice decorated the windowpane, inside and out. She couldn't see anything. Sam breathed on the glass, then used her palm to polish out a place to peer through.

What she saw made her wonder if she was really awake.

Like a snow sculpture come to life, the stallion floated along the riverbank.

Why was he there? Why was he so excited? Could the pony have joined the Phantom's wild band? Was Moon trying once more to rejoin the herd? Did the Phantom need her?

Sam breathed on the pane again. She rubbed so hard, her fingers made the glass squeak, but the glass was still too blurry to see through clearly. She had to go out there.

Moving silently, careful not to step on the loose board that creaked in the hallway, Sam started for the stairs.

"Samantha?" Dad's no-nonsense voice stopped her.

"Yes?" she whispered.

"Are you going down for a midnight snack?"

Sam didn't want to lie. Not only was she incredibly bad at it, she was pretty sure Dad had wakened to the same sound she had.

"Yes, Dad." Sam waited, but he didn't say anything else.

She tiptoed downstairs, grabbed an apple she didn't want from the fruit basket, and held it as she looked from the kitchen window.

The stallion had moved out of view. She might have been watching a photographic negative develop vague shapes of dark and light, picturing a bleak winter night.

She sighed. Her breath clouded the glass.

Still holding the apple, she went back upstairs.

"Sam? Just remember there's nothing that horse needs that you can give him. He was probably just saying hello."

"Okay," she said, but as she slid back into bed and pulled the blankets up to cover her nose, Sam knew her father was wrong.

* * *

The next morning at school, she cornered Jake.

He'd just slammed his locker, given the dial a spin, and glanced up when he saw her coming.

"Don't look at me like that," he muttered, and turned to go on his way.

"Don't make me pin you against the lockers," Sam threatened.

Jake's jaw dropped open and he did a quick comparison of their sizes and strength. She was just over five feet tall, and Jake claimed to be six feet, one inch. She had the lean fitness of a girl who worked with horses. Jake had broad shoulders and the determined look of the youngest of seven brothers.

"If you think you can do that, you're dreaming," he told her.

"That's what I want to talk with you about," Sam said. "Only it wasn't a dream, exactly."

Because they were at school, Sam didn't want to remind Jake too pointedly about his cougar dream. She watched his face to see if he understood her hint.

He did.

He leaned so close their foreheads nearly touched. "Every time I let you weasel something out of me, I'm sorry. Not everything is a sign. In fact, almost nothing is." He straightened and continued down the hall, looking frustrated as she fell into step beside him. "So, what do you want?"

Sam told him about the lost pony.

"Yeah, so?" He tried to look bored, but Sam

wasn't fooled. When she'd been a little girl, she'd called Jake's lively brown eyes "mustang eyes." Every now and then, he couldn't hide that sparkle of interest.

"So, knowing how cute you think Rachel is—"

"You just talked yourself out of a partner," Jake said.

Sam didn't remind him of the lingering looks he'd given Rachel, because she knew the truth. Jake thought Rachel was cute, but he didn't trust her. She also noticed he hadn't walked away.

"Jen's parents won't let her go with me for some reason—"

"Common sense would be my guess," Jake grumbled.

"—so if the cowboys from River Bend haven't found the pony by the time I get home, you could go looking with me."

"I'm your second choice, is what you're saying."

"Yeah, but you're a decent tracker," Sam teased.

As the bell rang, hurrying them toward class, Jake gave in.

"I'll go, but I'm doing it for the pony," he said.

"Not for Rachel?"

"Not for you. I'm only bringing you along for cougar bait."

"Ha ha," Sam said, but she didn't think Jake was a bit funny.

Chapter Seventeen

They found Chipper at Aspen Creek. Like a small shadow, he stood next to Moon, nosing at soggy leaves.

The shaggy Shetland lifted his head, gave a high-pitched nicker, then a snort. Moon returned the snort, but he didn't share Chipper's excitement. For every step Sam and Jake rode closer, Moon backed a step.

"He *is* a beauty," Jake said.

He'd said the same thing when they'd seen the young mustang before. Sam turned to look at Jake. The longing in his eyes surprised her.

"This time he's not gonna run." Jake kept his voice low as they rode closer. "You're not gonna leave your little buddy, are you, Moon?"

The black sidled away, eyes rolling white. He tossed his head in a come-with-me gesture. From birth, Moon had learned to flee humans. Only loyalty to this new herd member had kept him here this long.

Chipper didn't grasp why Moon kept moving up

the sidehill. The pony stood firm, as if setting a good example for his cowardly friend.

"I don't know why he has to go back," Sam whispered to Jake. "They're both happier this way."

Jake's fingers rested on his rope. He pretended he hadn't heard her, and Sam knew it wasn't worth an argument. And she knew why.

The pony would die in the wild. Moon might be injured protecting him. Even if they joined a wild band—and it was unlikely any stallion would let Moon close to his mares—the Shetland's short legs couldn't keep pace with the fleet mustangs.

Bitterbrush rustled as Moon moved past it. His front hooves struck, one-two, one-two, in a troubled dance. He wished Chipper would come along, and he gave a low nicker to tell him so.

Forelock flipping from side to side, the pony glanced between the riders and the uneasy young stallion. He jogged toward Moon. When he'd reached him, Chipper stretched his neck up. The tall stallion lowered his head and the horses touched noses.

Sam's heart squeezed in pity.

"Let's get this done," Jake muttered. "Head him toward me."

Sam urged Ace forward. Moon bolted out of reach of Jake's rope, but he paused, looking confused, when the pony didn't follow.

"He doesn't belong out here, and you do," Sam called. Moon pricked his ears to catch her voice while his eyes shifted to watch her take his only friend.

Jake was shaking out a loop of rope. He was about to lasso Chipper.

"Do you have to put a rope on him?" Sam asked.

Just then, the two horses' voices blended in a longing neigh.

"If we want him to choose us, I do."

Jake's rope sang out and settled gently over Chipper's neck. For an instant, the Shetland leaned back against the rope and flashed an insulted look. But when Jake wheeled Witch, the pony trotted along behind obediently.

Sam looked back. Moon moved in certain leaps up the hill, out of Aspen Creek canyon. The young stallion wouldn't endanger his freedom, even for his friend.

He's smart to see that, Sam thought, because it never would have worked out for the two buddies. Moon had been taught to flee and Chipper had been taught to follow.

They decided to take Chipper to River Bend and let Jed Kenworthy come pick him up with a trailer.

"It's too long a walk for your short little legs," Sam told Chipper.

Sam glanced down at the pony, then up to see Jake pretend his eyes hadn't been searching the terrain behind them.

"Is Moon following us?" she asked.

Jake shook his head. "No, and it's a good thing. We don't need another jug-headed mustang hanging around the ranch."

There it was again. Yearning tinged Jake's voice when he talked about Moon.

"What if you could have him?" Sam ignored Jake's groan of disgust. "He's so eager for a herd, I bet BLM will get him in one of their gathers."

The idea of the Phantom's son in captivity made her sick, but Jake worked magic with young horses.

"Your dad won't get another horse for us to work on till the doctor gives the okay." Jake rubbed the leg he'd broken just a month ago.

Dad and Jake used River Bend feed and facilities to care for horses that needed schooling. Jake did the training, and when the horses were sold or returned to their owners, Dad and Jake split the money. It was a great deal for everyone, but Sam knew Dad wouldn't bring in a new horse before Jake was completely recovered.

"I'm fine," Jake said, as if reading her mind. "I don't know what the doc's waiting for."

"Gee, d'you think he might have lost faith in your good judgment when you cut off your own cast?" Sam said.

Jake shrugged. He wasn't the impatient type, but nothing—not pain, doctor's orders, or his furious mother—had been able to keep him out of the saddle for more than a couple of weeks.

Dad and Dallas rode in over the River Bend bridge as Sam and Jake rode in through the back pastures. They met in the middle of the ranch yard and talked while everyone except Jake unsaddled their mounts.

"Looks like you caught the little critter," Dallas said.

As he watched Jake tether the pony to a hitching rail, Dallas swept off his hat and used his forearm to wipe his brow. It was cold, not hot, but the old fore-man looked tired.

"Down by Aspen Creek," Jake said.

"Are Pepper and Ross still out?" Sam asked.

"Naw, they took off for the holidays," Dad said. "They'll be back for the wedding, maybe."

Days ago, Sam had heard Dad offer the hands a vacation and heard them refuse.

"What changed their minds?" she asked.

"Your Gram convinced Pepper to call home. He left his folks in Idaho over a year ago." Dad shrugged with an understanding look. "After he talked to his mother, he decided to go, and Ross said he'd go along, too."

Sam was glad for Pepper, but she hoped his trip home was only a visit. They all liked the young cowboy. After Brynna had seen him work with Pop-corn and Mikki, she'd hoped Dad could spare him for the HARP program. If it ever got going.

"You don't think he'll stay in Idaho, do you?" Sam asked.

"Not much chance of that," Dallas answered. "His teeth were already chattering, thinking about the icicles that'd be hanging off his hat brim if his dad sends him out after strays."

The men were chuckling as Sam checked Ace's feet.

"Wow, poor boy." Sam touched a rock lodged against the wall of the gelding's hoof. She tried to pick it out with her fingers, but Ace jerked the hoof from her grasp. "Sore, huh, boy?"

Dad was beside Sam at once. He helped remove the rock, then held it up. The rock was no bigger than Sam's thumbnail, but one end was pointed.

"Ouch," Dad said. His expression was faintly accusing as he handed it to Sam. "Surprised you didn't notice that when it went in."

She thought over the ride out to Aspen Creek, their time with Moon, and the ride back. She shook her head.

"I don't think he reacted at all, Dad."

"Didn't see anything from where I was sittin'." Jake's voice was gruff as he swung back into Witch's saddle.

Even though Dad believed her, Sam was glad Jake had backed her up. From Jake, that amounted to praise, and she couldn't help smiling.

"Wish you'd been riding with us," Dallas said to Jake.

"Yeah?"

"We were tracking that cougar till the fog came in."

Sam stared through the ranch gates toward the range. A haze hung in the foothills leading up to the Calico Mountains.

It was probably *pogonip*. Dad said *pogonip* was a Native American word for the frozen fog that hung over Nevada's Great Basin.

This time of year, *pogonip* could hamper them for weeks. The first few days, it coated sagebrush and rocks and trees, making you think of a crystal fairyland. But later, it became a nuisance. Chores didn't stop just because you couldn't see more than a few yards ahead of your nose.

"There was a set of small tracks in with a mustang herd. We thought they might belong to him." Dad nodded toward Chipper. "The cat tracks were on top, as if he was going along behind, hoping for a straggler."

Sam swallowed. Dad and Dallas had to have been following the Phantom's herd. Yellowtail had two big mares, but the Phantom's herd had several foals and yearlings.

"Where were they going?" Sam asked.

Dad pointed. "Up there on those rocky shelves. With night coming on and the *pogonip*, we lost 'em." He gave a frustrated frown. "Mighta gone on up the switchbacks into the Calicos, or taken a trail into Lost Canyon. It'd be for the best if that cat stayed up there." He gave Sam a sympathetic smile. "Tough on mustangs, maybe, but better than having him down by the ranches."

Sam had to agree.

"Brynna said she was calling the Department of Wildlife, just to alert them," Dad said.

"Might ride up there tomorrow and take a look," Jake said, then he added, "since tomorrow's Saturday and I don't have anything else to do."

Dad took the hint with a smile. "How long before you can work raw stock again?"

"Doc says New Year's Day, 'if I behave myself.'"

When Jake mimicked the stern doctor, Sam laughed. Jake was so cool and responsible, it was easy to forget he was a kid, until something like this reminded her.

"Hang in there, Jake." Dad patted Witch on the shoulder. "It'll be over before you know it."

Even though Dad hadn't said or done anything sappy, Jake shifted in an embarrassed way. Then he touched his hat brim and galloped out of the yard.

"Jake Ely's a good kid," Dallas said, looking after him.

"Yeah," Dad agreed.

Sam liked Jake a lot, but hearing him praised made her uncomfortable. She didn't want people to expect too much of him.

Slowly, careful of his bruised hoof, Sam was leading Ace to his pen when Dad called after her.

"You can go with Jake tomorrow if you like, Sam."

"I can?" She swung around to meet Dad's eyes. Had he become a mind reader like Jake, or had he guessed how much she wanted to ride out and check the Phantom's herd? Maybe he'd decided she was a responsible young woman. Or maybe he was giving her permission before she brewed up an excuse to ride out there on her own.

"Unless you want to go with your Gram and me to Darton, where we'll pick out something decent for me to wear to the wedding." Dad rubbed the back of his neck.

Sam could hear the echo of Gram's voice in the *something decent*.

"I'd rather go to the dentist," Dallas muttered.

Dad smiled in agreement. "We're going to meet Brynna for a Chinese dinner at about five."

"Thanks, Dad," Sam said. "But I'm not in the mood for shopping."

Dad's gaze shifted toward the ten-acre pasture as if he were looking for something, but he'd heard her.

"Can't say I'm surprised," he said. "Since you'll need to rest Ace, I want you to ride Strawberry. She's sound, sensible, and she doesn't like cats. She'll give you plenty of warning if one's around."

Dad fixed her with a look that said he wasn't going to start lecturing. Sam felt proud of his faith in her.

"I'm trusting you to know what's smart and what's not, and to tell me if there's anything worth worrying about," he said.

"I will, Dad," Sam promised.

After the horses were bedded down, Dad, Sam, and Dallas walked up to the house together. With the other cowboys gone, Dallas had agreed to eat dinner with the family.

"Not that I'm going to make a regular thing of this," Dallas said, stomping off his boots before they entered Gram's kitchen.

"Only if you want to," Dad said. "I know you like your privacy."

Inside, Gram brandished lists of stores and magazine pages showing grooms' apparel, and the look on Dallas's face said he wasn't at all sure a home-cooked dinner was worth such fuss.

Dad kept an easygoing smile in place. He was in such a good mood, Sam got ready to ask if she could have one of the Elys' kittens.

Just then, Gram asked Dad if he'd picked out a best man. Sam guessed that was the male equivalent of a maid of honor.

"Think I need one?" Dad asked. When his eyes wandered to Dallas, the old cowboy pushed away from the table, stood, and headed for the door.

"Evenin'," he said, taking his hat from the hook. And then he left.

Dad laughed, and Sam thought he was taking the same advice he'd given Jake.

Hang in there, he'd said. *It'll be over before you know it.*

* * *

Sam kneeled on her patchwork quilt and set her alarm clock for seven A.M.

That wasn't exactly sleeping in, she thought, but it made a difference that she'd have the entire day to herself. She was about to slip under the covers when Gram tapped at her door, then bustled in.

Gram wore her red corduroy robe zipped almost to her chin. The long, gray braid hanging over her shoulder made her look young. Sam was glad to see her. She thought of all the nights Gram had come into her room to tuck her in, and wondered when she had stopped.

Tonight, Gram looked like she had something on her mind.

"You're happy about the wedding, aren't you, Gram?" Sam asked, and she felt her own smile puff up her cheeks.

"I am," Gram said, almost surprised. "I haven't seen your father this excited for a long time. I mean, he's not even fighting me about this shopping trip. That's definitely a first."

"I think it's going to work out fine," Sam said. Her amazement was an echo of Gram's.

A warm hug, filled with the scent of Gram's lilac bath powder, engulfed Sam. She closed her eyes and enjoyed it.

"Oh, wait," Gram said. She drew back and pushed her hand into her bathrobe pocket. Paper rustled. "I have been so absentminded, thinking of all the wedding details, I forgot to give you this yesterday."

Gram held out an envelope. "From Mikki, it looks like."

Sam snapped on her bedside lamp and took the letter.

"It is from her," Sam said. Mikki hadn't written since she'd graduated from the HARP program, and Sam had never heard of Citruswood, California, but Mikki's real name was Michelle Small, and that's what it said in the return address. "I wonder why the envelope's so lumpy?"

"I'll leave you alone to solve that mystery," Gram said.

She kissed Sam's forehead. "Are you sure you won't change your mind about going to the mall?"

"I'm sure," Sam said. "Good night."

She was burning with curiosity. As the door closed behind Gram, Sam had already slipped her fingertip along the envelope's flap to pop it loose.

Chapter Eighteen

Sam pulled her nightgown down to cover her ankles as she sat cross-legged on her patchwork quilt. She took a deep breath, then slipped the piece of blue-lined notebook paper from the envelope and unfolded it. Something fell out.

The loop was almost weightless as it hit her lap, but the light from Sam's bedside lamp made it glow like something magical.

And, in a way, it was magical.

The horsehair bracelet shone in many shades of silver. Just a few months ago, Sam had braided it from strands of the Phantom's mane. Now, she cradled it in the cup of one hand and closed her eyes for a few seconds. Then she kissed it for luck and slipped it over her right hand.

The bracelet warmed her wrist. Sam knew that was impossible. She stared at the bracelet. Some strands were icy white like a unicorn's horn. A few shone black as dragons' scales. Most shimmered like melted silver, the color of the Phantom's coat by moonlight.

With her other hand, Sam turned the bracelet on her wrist. It seemed to vibrate at her touch.

Was she dreaming or hypnotizing herself?

Sam shook her head. Weird. Too weird.

To shake off the feeling, she opened the folded piece of paper and began to read Mikki's letter.

Dear Sam,

How are you? I'm doing fine, but I miss you and Popcorn and I have 86 school days until summer. I hope you guys do the HARP program again!!!

Here goes the real reason I wrote. Don't take this wrong, ok, but I think you need the bracelet back. Ms. Olson phoned and mentioned about the Phantom getting stolen and treated so bad by Karla Starr. And about how the Phantom hardly ever comes around any more and even when he does, he doesn't really trust you. That is so awful.

I'm not so stupid that I think bad stuff is happening because I took the bracelet. Still, if you had a chance to get near HIM again, and you were wearing the bracelet, what could it hurt? And it might help.

So good luck. Please write back.

Your friend?

Mikki

Sam read the letter over one more time before slipping it back into its envelope, setting it on her bedside table, and turning off her lamp. She slid under the covers, but her eyes wouldn't close.

She stared at her bedroom wall. She could remember the late September afternoon she'd given the bracelet to Mikki, but she couldn't remember why.

Mikki had led Popcorn out to lure Dark Sunshine home, though the mare really wanted to return to the Phantom. Mikki's calm skill with Popcorn had soothed both horses, and later Sam had given her the bracelet. She'd told Mikki it wasn't enchanted, or anything like that, but that it stood for something.

What did it stand for? Sam rolled the silver circlet up and down her arm, thinking.

The horsehair bracelet was a bond, Sam decided. It was proof the stallion had let her stand beside him, finger-combing his mane over and over again.

Sam turned on one side and closed her eyes.

Under the covers, the horsehair prickled against her wrist. She decided the bracelet was a symbol, a lot like a wedding ring. This symbol said that she and the Phantom trusted each other.

Twice before, the Phantom had put himself between Sam and danger. Now it was her turn to help him.

If the cougar was stalking the Phantom's herd, she'd call Brynna at once.

* * *

The next morning, Sam stayed in bed while Gram and Dad bustled around. She listened for the phone to ring, hoping Jake would call to tell her where to meet him.

By the time Dad and Gram drove away, he still hadn't called. Sam dressed in layers so she'd be able to peel them off as the day warmed up. Her lined leather coat would be warmest, but it looked too much like deer hide. She was not going to tempt that cougar to pounce on her.

"In fact," Sam mumbled to herself, "I have just the thing to convince him I'm not good to eat."

Sam dug through her bottom drawer. At last her fingers grazed a bunch of bumpy knit wool. She tugged out a hat and a long fringed scarf. Aunt Sue had knitted them several years ago. As Gram had pointed out when Sam whispered how homely they were, Aunt Sue didn't have many domestic skills, but she was still a wonderful, loving aunt.

Yes, she is, Sam thought. The screeching orange-red was not a color found in nature. If cougars saw in color, this would assure them she wasn't prey.

Perfect. She carried Aunt Sue's creations downstairs.

The kitchen clock said seven thirty when she stood sipping orange juice and eating the biscuits Gram had left in the oven. Jake still hadn't called.

Could he and Witch already be here, waiting for her in the yard? Sam peered through the window at the overcast morning. They weren't.

It was nearly eight o'clock when she dialed the

Elys' telephone number. She really hated doing it. Although Mrs. Ely was one of the nicest people Sam knew, she was also her history teacher, and it felt awkward to call.

This time, she needn't have worried. Sam quit counting when the phone had rung eleven times.

Jake hadn't said exactly when he was going. Maybe he'd left really early and decided not to call her. After all, he'd already started for home when Dad told her that she could go.

Sam's thermal shirt grated the horsehair bracelet against her wrist as she put on her parka. Without a mirror to show her how silly she looked, she pulled on the neon-orange hat and wrapped the scarf around her throat.

She'd just have to find Jake out there.

Sam decided to check out Lost Canyon first. Jake didn't know how to find the Phantom's hidden valley in the Calico Mountains, so he'd probably headed this way. Besides, it was closer, and the *pogonip* wasn't as thick in this direction.

She could see through it pretty well. The frozen fog was no more than a blur before her eyes as she searched for signs of the mustangs and the cougar.

Watching Jake track was different than doing it herself. He made it look easy. So did Witch. The roached-maned mare was used to Jake's leaning low, moving from one side of the saddle to the other. Strawberry wasn't.

At first, the pink-roan mare was just glad to be on

the range. Strawberry loped, neck arched, across War Drum Flats. She responded to each stirring of Sam's legs or hands, jogging up the mustang shortcut and crowding through the tall brush. But when Sam reined her in, then leaned down to look for a cluster of hoofprints, the mare turned skittish.

"I'm not going to fall, girl," Sam assured the mare. "And they didn't come this way, at least not lately."

She made Strawberry stand for a minute.

First, Sam looked up. There were no cliffs overhead from which a cougar could launch himself. That was good.

Surveying the range from this height would show her Jake, if he was nearby. Wisps of fog hid some gulches, but they couldn't cloak a horse and rider. Nothing moved down there. Even the cattle were far to the north.

Jake must have ridden into Lost Canyon, expecting her to follow him. That's what she'd told Dad she'd do, and he was trusting her to keep her word.

"C'mon, girl," Sam said, and Strawberry obeyed.

After an hour of riding, squinting into shadows, and gazing up at the tops of boulders, always alert for the cougar, Sam's shoulders ached and her hands were shaky. She looked down at her watch and couldn't believe it was only ten thirty.

The last thing she'd recognized had been the cracked rock with water seeping through it. She'd noticed it right after she entered Lost Canyon.

Sam forced Strawberry to hug the right side of

the trail, since the left dropped off to thin air. It was weird. She knew the stunning view of sandstone cliffs was out there. She should have been able to look down on the Phantom's herd, if the mustangs had returned here. But she saw only swirling fog.

Sam listened. Faintly, she heard the whisper of water. The turquoise stream was down there somewhere. She kept riding.

It was a good thing she knew where she was going. She looked up for cougars and down for tracks, but *pogonip* fog hid most everything but the trail underfoot. Even that looked eerie. Rock and dirt sparkled as if they'd been sprinkled with iridescent confetti. The sheen must have been from ice crystals, but Strawberry's footing stayed sure.

"There!" Sam said finally.

Strawberry started at the sound of her voice. Sam reined her in, rubbed the mare's neck to comfort her, then studied the ground.

Highlighted by the frost, a single set of hoofprints advanced before her. They must be from Witch. That meant Jake was just ahead of her.

Sam sighed. She hadn't realized how worried she'd been about the possibility of being all alone. Now she knew she wasn't. The tracks turned off the main trail, and she recognized the sudden slant. Here, Brynna had turned Jeep down a deer trail that led through sparse, green vegetation.

The stream sounded louder, as if it were shushing her, cautioning her to be quiet. How far ahead was

Jake? She wanted to call his name, but Strawberry was already nervous. What if her voice startled Witch into putting a foot wrong? She remembered how Jeep had stumbled, and decided not to risk it.

Before, she'd trusted Ace to navigate this path. Now, she had to trust Strawberry.

It wasn't easy. The mare's gait had turned choppy. She took two ambling steps, then flung up her head and listened. Her ears flicked forward, to the sides, then lay flat. Next, she bounded into the middle of the trail and turned her head from side to side.

"The fog's got you worried, doesn't it, girl? I don't like it either, but it's just air and water. We're fine."

Sam felt the saddle shift as if the mare's muscles had loosened. They moved ahead, and Sam was just wondering how close they were to the canyon floor when Strawberry lunged to the right. Sam's shoulder struck the sandstone wall beside her. Strawberry stopped and snorted.

From somewhere in the fog, a horse returned the snort.

"Jake?" Sam shivered. Her voice didn't fly out and echo. The fog formed a wall. She might have called from inside a closet.

"Okay, Strawberry. It feels like we're almost down. And there's a horse out there. Whether it's Witch or one of the mustangs, you can work by scent a lot better than I can. Finding them is up to you."

Sam firmed her legs around the mare, asking her to step out a little faster.

Strawberry didn't have a chance to obey.

Sudden impact, like a pillowcase full of sand, struck Sam's shoulders and yanked her back over Strawberry's rump. Gasping, strangling, her throat burning, she flew into a backward somersault and rolled. The noose around her throat released, and she fell facedown on rock. She pushed herself up. The world swirled in sickening flashes of color. Wobbling on her hands and knees, she fought dizziness.

Suddenly Sam knew what had happened. *The cougar.*

She forced her knees to straighten. Standing, she staggered forward and almost stepped on him.

Its mouth full of the orange-red scarf, the cat batted at his mouth with a huge paw. Hissing and growling, he fought to free his teeth from the loose knit.

As the cat shook his head and coughed, Sam heard Strawberry's hooves retreating up the path, out of the arroyo.

Don't look like prey.

Sam grabbed the sides of her unzipped parka and flapped them like giant wings.

The cat watched her. His amber eyes narrowed, then widened. He smelled like wet laundry. He panted. Tongue and teeth working at the scarf, he still studied her, gauging her strength. Beneath his hide, Sam saw the pumping of his ribs. The young cat was half starved.

If she didn't scare him away, he would eat her.

Sam growled. She jumped in place. The path was

wide here, and even if she fell, it would be better than being ripped by those fangs.

She saw those fangs now, because the cat had fought free of her scarf. With a swing of his paw, he batted the scarf away and settled into a crouch.

Don't let him see your back. Instinct told Sam to run, but her brain insisted that was wrong.

Rush him, her brain ordered her shaking legs. *Chase him. It's your only chance.*

She did it. Hollering and running, she kicked at the cougar's curled toes. He jerked one paw back with a yowl, then turned almost into himself, tawny body bent in half.

His thick, black-tipped tail struck her shins, and suddenly he ran up the trail and was gone.

"Go! Get out of here! Bad cat!" Screaming until her throat was sore, Sam backed away from the spot where the cougar had taken its stand.

She was lucky to be alive. Holding one hand against the rock wall for support, she kept backing toward Arroyo Azul. She didn't know how to get home from the arroyo floor, but anything was better than going up.

The cougar was gone. She was sure of it, but she wouldn't go toward him, and she would not turn her back.

"He's got the hang of hunting," she mumbled. "I don't think he'll starve. If I hadn't been wearing Aunt Sue's ugly scarf . . ."

Sam stopped talking to herself. That couldn't be

normal. She had no one to depend on but herself.

"Get a grip," she ordered, then closed her lips hard.

Sam's head felt so heavy, she might have been balancing a bowling ball on her weary neck.

Black dots frenzied in front of her eyes. This wasn't what Dad had meant when he'd said she should do what she knew was right.

Except . . . it was. She'd looked for Jake. She'd watched for the cougar. And she'd scared it away!

Shivering, she stopped to zip her parka. The only warm thing on her entire body was the wrist circled by her silver horsehair bracelet. That wasn't enough.

She touched her head. Amazingly, she still wore the odd little hat, so she stretched it to cover her ears. She wouldn't tempt hypothermia. Down in Arroyo Azul, it should get warmer.

Her back ached as if she were carrying a hundred-pound backpack. Was this how it felt to be in shock? If so, how was she supposed to deal with it?

Think.

Hooves sounded behind her.

"Jake!" Sam yelled, but she kept backing. "Why didn't you come help me? Did you see it? All your tracking skills . . . What if something's above you leaping around from rock to rock, looking down, just waiting for a chance to bite your neck?"

Sam heard her voice echo. Below her boots, the dirt turned level. She smelled mud, grass, and horses. And then she heard a familiar nicker.

Chapter Nineteen

Sam stood on the floor of the arroyo.

The *pogonip* had thinned to a faint shimmer in the air. An earthen floor spread away from her. She had left the cougar on the mountain. She was sure of that, because here there was nowhere for him to hide.

The low nicker came again, and finally Sam dared to look over her shoulder. In the distance, she saw dark shapes. She turned and walked toward them.

Wild horses moved in a cautious herd, seeking ground a little farther away. But right before her was their king.

The Phantom stood in the turquoise stream. Mist swirled around him as he walked to the riverbank.

Sam's feet moved. She didn't tell them to, but they carried her toward the stallion.

He lowered his head, watching Sam come closer. His neck curved so he could face her. His silver hide wrinkled like silk, except in that one place where he'd been scarred by a rope.

Sam stopped walking.

The Phantom stood just a few feet away, near enough to hear her whisper.

Sam tried to say his secret name, but she only croaked. She swallowed. Her throat had been working a minute ago. She'd been talking to herself, hadn't she?

The stallion tossed his forelock free of concerned brown eyes. Sam reached out a hand, telling him not to worry.

Prancing like a colt, he danced in the stream, sprinkling her with drops of water. Sam let them hit her face. The moisture felt good. Why was her face so hot? Maybe she really was in shock. Maybe the silver stallion was a fever dream and she was still alone up on that trail.

No. It wasn't a dream.

The Phantom was greeting her just as he used to before the rodeo. Just as he'd come to her in the river the first night she'd moved back from San Francisco. Just as he had when he was Blackie, the colt she'd mounted in La Charla river, years ago.

It was happening all over again. And it was real.

"Jake always made me wait for a sign you were ready," Sam managed to whisper. The stallion stood, still and alert, so she kept talking. "In those days, you'd lower your head so I could slip the bridle over your nose, remember? And then you'd dance, waiting for me to swing onto your pretty back."

Chills rained down Sam's arms as the stallion

lowered his head and stamped a shower of stream water. Could he have understood every word?

He was asking her to ride him.

Sam caught her breath, daring to hope. But what if he wasn't? What if she tried, and fell, drenched herself, and had to spend the night here, soaked and waiting for rescue? Then she really would get hypothermia.

Even worse than that, what if she scared him so much he abandoned her forever?

Sam's shoulders sagged. Her knees buckled. She lowered herself to the ground. It was cold, but she didn't care. She couldn't have stood another minute.

The weakness was from the attack. She'd had the scare of her life. But the tears filling her eyes were from indecision. More than anything, she wanted to believe the stallion had forgiven her for what other men had done.

"You have to tell me, boy." She smooched, and his ears swiveled to her voice again. "Do you trust me? You can, you know. And if you carry me out of here on some secret wild horse path, I'll never tell anyone. Not in a million years."

He splashed closer. One hoof pawed the bank, then he thrust his nose at her, lifting her arm with a sharp jerk. Sam reached out her hand and the stallion touched it with his nose.

His muzzle felt like velvet.

He was telling her she could do it, but should

she? Had he learned to trust only her and not other humans who'd harm him? The stallion nuzzled her hand, seeking more of her touch.

He'd learned. He knew she was the only one.

"Zanzibar," Sam whispered. Her voice was growing rusty again, but the stallion's silver ears flicked to catch every word. "It might only happen once, here in this arroyo. I'm going to do it."

She wobbled to her feet. The stallion walked in slow steps away from her, but he kept looking back to be sure she followed. Finally, he stopped and Sam saw two flat rocks. They formed stepping stones between her and the stallion.

Stream water rushed over them, making them slippery, but she wouldn't have to wade. One long step took her to the first rock and a shorter step took her to the next one.

"The only thing, boy, is that you're facing the wrong way."

Sam laughed. She rubbed her forehead in frustration, then stared at the small smear of blood on her hand.

"Okay, pretty horse," Sam said, moving into position. "I can't expect you to do everything."

The Phantom tossed his head in a nod. How could she keep him happy? Months ago, when he'd first come to her, she'd sung "Silent Night" and he'd loved it.

"Well, the season's right," Sam told him. "If I sing,

will you put up with my clumsiness?"

Sam sang and the river accompanied her, but the song was jerky and the rock too slippery. When Sam tried to fling her belly over his back, the Phantom skittered away two steps and she nearly crashed into the icy water.

Both arms out for balance, she watched the horse.

"All right," she said, panting from the exertion. "It's okay."

The stallion's ears flicked at her breathless voice. His silver hide shivered and his tail switched with impatience. She had one more chance to get it right.

"I've got to remember how Jake taught me to do this, and I've got to remind you." Sam closed her eyes, turned her face up to the pale sun and remembered.

In memory, summer banished the river's snowmelt. Eyes still closed, Sam stood as she should have the first time. Shoulder to shoulder with the stallion, she faced his tail, with her left palm tented over his warm withers.

Think summer, Sam told herself, and the cramped muscles in her legs seemed to stretch. She lifted her sodden right boot from the water and swung it toward the horse, then away. When he didn't shy, she did it again.

"This is what it looks like, remember? I throw this leg over and the other one lifts off, and—" Sam's voice caught. How could she have forgotten this part? "And I kiss the far side of your neck before I straighten up and ride you away."

She opened her eyes, breaking the trance of memory.

This couldn't be done in a tangle of arms and legs. It had to be a single movement, fluid and graceful.

She let her fingers move on his withers. That left hand wasn't meant to lever her up. It was there to steady them both.

The Phantom's muzzle nudged her spine. He was ready.

Sam swung her right leg. Its arc cleared the stallion's back and lifted her left leg from the river water. Momentum made her right leg hit the stallion's far side. Her stomach rested on his neck and — there! — she kissed the right side of his neck, then pushed herself, trembling, upright.

"Oh, my gosh, boy," Sam said through chattering teeth. "It's really happening. I love you, Zanzibar."

Gooseflesh raced up her arms and down again. She was cold and confused, and more excited than she'd ever been before.

She leaned forward, rested her cheek on the stallion's mane, and the confusion faded away. Her arms hung and her hands trailed like rain on his silken neck. The Phantom shivered, but he didn't move until Sam sat tall.

The stallion's head came up as she straightened.

"We've done this before, boy."

Sam balanced and held a lock of mane in her left

hand. Her trembling right hand rested on her thigh. She sighted ahead, through the stallion's curved silver ears.

"Here we go, boy."

Before she tightened her legs, the Phantom took a step, testing, then stopped. Sam kept her fingers wound in his mane, but she smoothed her other hand over his shoulder.

"I remember this, don't you?" Sam said, and then she leaned forward.

The stallion moved down the stream. A few curious nickers followed them, but the Phantom trembled with the memories. Strength coursed through every muscle. It was clear to Sam that the great stallion was letting her command him. For now.

He lurched left. Sam grabbed his mane with both hands as the stallion vaulted onto the bank and leaped into a lope.

Ohmygosh, ohmygosh, don't gallop. Every inch of her body trembled. She was not a good bareback rider. She didn't want to fall. Something black showed in the rock wall ahead.

The stallion entered a tunnel. She ducked her head, but then the Phantom slowed to a walk and her head snapped back.

Sam took a shuddering breath. *I'm okay. We're fine. This might never happen again. I'm not afraid. I'm in heaven.*

This tunnel wasn't as dark as the one that led to the stallion's hideaway in the Calico Mountains. Could it be part of the same passageway? Excitement made it hard to think.

The ceiling was so low, the stallion dropped his head to the level of his chest. Sam flattened on the stallion's neck and still the rock grated against her back.

Light flickered through cracks in the stone walls. It gave their journey a strange underwater feel, until Sam's eyes focused on the wall on her right.

Horses. Drawings of rust-red horses marked the wall. They looked like they'd been drawn by a second grader. And then Sam realized what they were. Petroglyphs. The drawings had been made by ancient tribes. Maybe they'd been daubed by Paiutes or Shoshones, or by families before there even were tribes.

Sam knew one thing for sure: Horses and people had lived together in this valley many, many years ago.

Sam felt a warmth in her chest. She must be the only person alive who knew this tunnel. By the time she tried to tie the drawings into some sort of story, they were gone.

The light at the end of the tunnel grew bright.

"Thank you, boy," she whispered to the stallion.

He stopped. Then, to Sam's horror, his back legs lashed out.

"Easy, boy."

The stallion gave a snort and kicked out again. This time, his legs twisted, loosening the grip of her legs. He wanted her off. Now.

"Zanzibar, I understand."

Holding tight to his mane, she slipped from his back. Her feet had just reached the stone floor when the stallion began backing away. His head bowed. His mane rushed forward to veil his face. He was going . . .

Suddenly dizzy, Sam braced her hands against the side of the tunnel. Silence claimed the air around her. When her senses stopped spinning, she focused on the spot where the Phantom had been. There was nothing but blackness.

Now she began to shiver seriously. She rubbed her hands up and down her parka arms, hearing the skid of her abraded palms on the nylon. She turned her back on the dark tunnel.

"Walk," she ordered herself. Then she heard another voice.

She jogged toward the light as fast as she could without falling. She didn't know where this tunnel ended and she didn't care, because somewhere ahead, she heard Jake calling her name.

The mouth of the tunnel opened behind a rock. Sam had to climb, pulling herself up with painfully cold hands. This couldn't be the way the horses exited. Following the light must have led her away from the mustangs' path.

Her heart vaulted up, rejoicing. She wouldn't give away their secret.

"Good! Oh, good!" Sam chuckled as she lowered herself toward a gravelly path. Her feet shot out from under her, and she rode a dirt slide down the face of a foothill.

Jake was sitting on Witch, holding Strawberry's reins, gawking at her.

Sam staggered to her feet. She brushed at the seat of her jeans and looked over her shoulder.

"I think I slid through the denim," she said, giggling.

"I think you're hysterical." Jake dropped Strawberry's reins, ground-tying her, then moved to stand in front of Sam.

"Hey, you weren't down there, were you?" she asked.

"Down where?"

"In Arroyo Azul?"

Jake shook his head.

"But then, who was?" Sam asked. "I was following the tracks of a single horse down through Lost Canyon, past the overlook, and down into the arroyo."

"Sam, I called your house this morning and no one answered. Tell me what happened."

She covered her mouth to keep from laughing. She was feeling giddy, which really didn't make sense. *What happened?* It was kind of a lot to cover. She'd had the most terrifying moment of her life and the most wonderful. Part of it she'd never tell anyone, but she numbered off the three events on her fingers.

"First, I was following the horses. Then, the cougar attacked me. Last, Strawberry ran away."

"The cougar—" Delicately, Jake turned her so that he could see her back.

"Jake, don't look at my pants. I ripped the seat out—"

Jake's hand fell away from her shoulder. He turned awfully quiet, even for him.

Feeling embarrassed, Sam looked up at Jake's frozen face. Then she stared at his fingers, which held a tiny white feather.

"The goose down in your jacket is floating out through claw rips in the nylon," he said softly.

"My parka's wrecked?" Sam asked.

Jake stared at her as if she'd missed the point.

"Can you ride?" he asked.

"Of course I can ride." Sam snatched Strawberry's trailing reins, jammed her boot toe in the stirrup, and swung aboard. "If you only *knew* how I can ride," she muttered to herself.

She kicked Strawberry into a gallop. Jake shouted and Witch came thundering after the other mare.

Sam hated to make Jake worry, and she hated to run away from the magical hour she'd had with the Phantom. Most of all, she hated going home, but that was why she had to hurry before she lost her nerve.

Once there, she would have to tell Brynna the truth about the young cougar. When she did, there was a very good chance someone would go to Lost Canyon and shoot him.

Chapter Twenty

Sam had managed to ease her aching body out of bed by noon on Sunday. Trying not to move more muscles than she had to, she dressed to go over to Jen's house.

So far, she'd managed to get her underwear and socks on, but now came her jeans. She wasn't sure she was up to the challenge.

Her muscles weren't all that had suffered. Why were her memories of yesterday afternoon so blurry?

Before she went out in public, Sam thought she should try to remember what had happened after she'd met up with Jake.

She was pretty sure that she'd called Brynna the minute she got home. She'd confessed every detail of the cougar attack, but Brynna hadn't even let her finish. She'd insisted on speaking to Jake. Then she'd talked Jake through an embarrassing evaluation of Sam's physical condition.

Jake had checked her joints, the pupils of her eyes, and a bunch of other things, then Brynna had made him promise to stay with Sam until Wyatt and Gram came home. Brynna had given Jake ten minutes to put up the horses while she kept Sam on the phone.

The good news Brynna shared was that the cougar's future might not be as bleak as Sam feared. The Division of Wildlife planned to transplant him to a remote area of the Ruby Mountains, far east of the Calicos.

After that conversation, Sam remembered eating the soup and toast Jake forced on her. Then she'd spent an hour in the bathtub. The warm water had soaked some of the soreness out of the muscles that had been smacked by the weight of the cougar.

At least, she'd *thought* they had.

Now, Sam held on to her bedpost. With one leg in her jeans, the next one should be easy, right?

What she'd really wanted yesterday was to take a nap. But Jake had made her rest on the couch, where he could shake her awake and check her pupils whenever she happened to doze.

Sam remembered Dad waking her when he returned home from Darton, to ask if she wanted Chinese food. She didn't.

A few minutes later Brynna woke her and reminded her of the final fitting of their dresses at the Kenworthys' house, just in case she'd forgotten. She had.

When the phone rang at what must have been seven o'clock, though it felt like midnight, Gram had made Sam talk to Jen. Sam had felt groggy, and probably hadn't sounded excited when Jen revealed that Ryan, Rachel's twin, had arrived at the Gold Dust Ranch and was "way cute."

"Ta da!" Sam gave herself a fanfare as she zipped her jeans, but when her gaze shifted to the sweater waiting on her bed, she bit her lip.

"Honey, would you like some help with that?" Gram asked, poking her head around the corner of Sam's door.

"I feel like a baby. But yes, please," Sam said.

Gram was quick and gentle, but Sam gasped at the contortions required to get the sweater on.

"I can't figure out why I'm so sore." She groaned.

"That cougar hit you with over a hundred hungry pounds! Then he pulled you backward by your neck and you fell from the height of a horse!" Gram's hands shook as she arranged Sam's sweater. "'Sakes, Samantha, of course you're sore."

Sam nodded, then looked in the mirror. The idea of lifting a hairbrush made her wince. Her hair didn't look too bad. Maybe she'd just leave it as it was.

"Can you come downstairs and take some aspirin?" Dad asked from the doorway.

"Sure, I can."

"And have some breakfast before we leave for the Kenworthys'," Gram added. "If you don't feel better after that, we're going to see the doctor."

"But—" Sam began.

"No argument." Dad's voice rolled behind him as he started downstairs. "And if you two get over there and need some help getting home, call me."

"Of course, Wyatt," Gram said, following him down the stairs.

They left Sam so she could try her legs without an audience.

Walking like she was ninety-three instead of thirteen, Sam made it to the kitchen. Hot oatmeal with brown sugar and cream slid down her abused throat and warmed her from the inside out.

"Gram, this is great." She sighed.

She drained her orange juice glass and asked for a refill. When that was gone, Sam couldn't wait to get over to Jen's house.

Something was going on at the Gold Dust Ranch.

A teal-and-white-striped tent fluttered in the open area leading up to the Slocums' mansion.

"Has the circus come to town?" Sam asked.

"You might say that." Gram parked in front of the Kenworthys' cabin, next to Brynna's white truck. "Helen said that Linc came home from New York with big plans. He's entertaining 'investors' with a Western-style dinner in that heated tent."

Inch by inch, Sam climbed out of the car, and she stood for a moment before walking to the house.

"Yum," she said, taking a breath. The crisp air held more than the scent of sagebrush. Could that be barbecuing chicken inside that tent?

"Linc told Helen he couldn't trust this dinner to local cooks, so he flew in a team of chefs. I bet that's them." Gram nodded at a pair of white-coated men scurrying from the tent to the mansion. "Last I heard, the menu included smoked quail on nests of shoestring potatoes."

"It smells good," Sam admitted, but the word *investors* stuck in her mind. Linc Slocum's schemes had a way of turning sour in a hurry.

The door to the cabin swung open and Jen stood in the doorway.

"I won't give you a hug," she said, eyeing Sam.

"She's doing fine." Gram steadied Sam's elbow as they went inside.

The cozy living room was strewn with material and clothes and platters of food. Brynna stood in the midst of it, grinning.

"I thought that since we're an all-girl crew today," she said, "we could test recipes as well as model clothes."

Though she'd just finished breakfast, Sam thought it sounded like a great idea.

"Jed's out riding the fence line," Lila said, gesturing toward the mountains. "With the gourmet hoopla outside and the pinning and primping inside, he thought he'd just be in the way."

"Try one of these," Brynna encouraged, holding a plate of pastries toward Sam. "Better yet, take them with you to Jen's room. She can help you try on your dress. Tell me if you like the brown sugar or blueberry tarts best."

Jen grabbed the plate before Sam could, then guided her down the hall.

"I know how to find your room," Sam muttered.

"I'm not going to let you fall or something," Jen grumbled. "It's just like you to get attacked by a wild animal while I'm not around to watch."

"Sorry," Sam said. She knew Jen was covering her concern with sarcasm.

Sam struggled with her sweater. Stuck midway, looking through the burgundy knit, she recalled the last time she'd worn it. The day she'd tried to help Rachel pick a horse, the sweater had made her feel out of place. Today, Sam was surrounded by friends who cared about her, not what she was wearing. Or not wearing.

Finally free of the sweater and jeans, Sam turned toward the bridesmaid dress.

"Ouch." Jen gasped.

"Does it look that bad?" Sam wanted to hide whatever Jen had seen, but rushing didn't seem possible.

"I don't know how you can even—" Jen broke off, shaking her head. "Sam, your neck's probably too sore to look over your shoulder into the mirror—"

"I'm not even going to try." Sam stepped into the dress, but she couldn't seem to lift it as far as her hips.

"I guess you're lucky his claws and teeth didn't break the skin. If they had . . ." Jen shook her head. "I bet you'd be in the hospital getting pumped full of antibiotics. Still, you're black-and-blue from your neck down to the backs of your knees."

"It feels like it," Sam said.

"Did Brynna see?" Jen asked.

"Probably. I was pretty out of it last night. The whole county could have looked and I wouldn't have noticed."

"No wonder you're walking funny," Jen said. "Let me help you with the dress. And tomorrow, if you go to school—"

"Of course I'm going to school!"

"Anyhow, I'll carry your backpack."

"Thanks, Jen, you're the best."

"Oh, yeah, right." She shrugged off the compliment and zipped the dress. "Gosh, it looks perfect."

As Sam faced the mirror, Jen arranged the long forest-green skirts, then stepped back.

"Can you see my bruises?" Sam asked.

Jen brushed at the back of Sam's hair, smoothing it over her nape. "Hardly. You look amazing. Let's go show the others."

A chorus of sighs wafted their way. They entered the living room in time to see Brynna twirling the skirt of her bridal gown.

"Wow." Sam sighed. How could a few yards of satin and lace transform a hardworking outdoors-woman into a fairy-tale princess?

"It's not finished," Mrs. Coley said, her arms crossed and a huge smile on her face. "But when it is, I think it will do nicely."

"I love it!" Brynna hugged Mrs. Coley in thanks, then hurried to Sam and kissed her cheek.

"This calls for a toast," said Lila. "I have hot apple cider on the stove."

A knock sounded at the door before Lila took a step. It was quiet until Mrs. Coley whispered, "If it's a disaster with the investors, I'm not here."

"I am!" Jen said. "This could be fun."

Sam giggled and followed Jen. She didn't know whether to credit the brown sugar tarts or the friendship, but all at once she felt a whole lot better.

"Hello? Pardon me for interrupting, but I'm looking for Ms. Olson. Is she here?"

The English accent and coffee-colored hair proved the guy at the door was Ryan Slocum, Rachel's brother. Sam had to agree with Jen. So far, the male twin was a lot more appealing than the female.

He waited. Sam wondered if he thought they were both simpleminded, since neither she nor Jen had managed an answer, when Brynna came to the door.

"Yes?" In spite of her white lace gown, Brynna's tone was all business.

Ryan looked relieved. "Ah, Ms. Olson. I was told you're something of a wildlife expert."

Brynna nodded.

"Yes, well, if you'd be kind enough to come with me, I'd like your opinion on a situation in the dining tent." He nodded toward the billowing structure.

"I'm hopeless when it comes to food," Brynna said, looking confused.

"Food *is* the root of the problem—however, there's something else." He looked so perplexed, Brynna followed him outside.

Sam tucked in right behind them, holding her skirts clear of the cold ground. She should have taken time to slip on shoes, but this sounded too intriguing to miss.

Jen would have followed, too, if Lila hadn't snagged her elbow.

"The thing is," Ryan confided to Brynna, "I'd like to set a plan in action before I notify my father."

Ryan Slocum had his dad all sized up, Sam was thinking. But then she heard the crash of plates and a growl.

"Stay back," Brynna said. She pulled aside the flap of the tent, then glanced at Sam. "Go get my hand-held radio from the truck."

Although curiosity consumed her, Sam went. Every freezing-cold, bone-jarring step hurt, but she ran.

She returned, handed Brynna her radio, then edged closer to the tent. As she reached for the flap,

Sam could have sworn she heard the sound of purring.

And then Ryan moved in front of her.

"I'm not sure that gown is quite the thing for lion taming."

Sam stared at him in disbelief. He was blocking her way. Who did he think he was?

"That lion and I have already met," Sam assured Ryan, and while he tried to figure that out, she stepped right on by.

The cougar crouched on a linen-covered table that ran the length of the tent. Places had already been set with silver and china. Small cooked birds were centered on each plate.

Licking his whiskers and purring, the cougar made his way down the table, grabbing and swallowing with obvious pleasure.

Brynna's arm circled Sam's shoulders. To keep from disturbing the cat, she spoke next to Sam's ear.

"Division of Wildlife is on its way."

Sam nodded, and then, at the sound of approaching footsteps, she and Brynna glanced up to see Linc Slocum puffing toward the tent.

Sam felt sick. "You won't let him—"

"—do a single thing," Brynna promised.

Sam believed her. For a lady in a wedding dress, Brynna looked pretty tough.

As they watched from the front of the tent and the two uniformed chefs watched from the back, the cougar edged forward without wrinkling the linen tablecloth. He lashed out a paw, swept a green salad aside, then gulped another smoked quail.

"It's sort of amazing," Sam whispered. "Gram was right about bad deeds coming home to roost."

Close by, Linc was yelling, while his son spoke in low, reasonable tones.

"If Linc hadn't killed that cougar's mom," Sam continued, "I bet that cat would be up in the Calicos chasing mule deer instead of down here, wrecking Linc's party."

The Division of Wildlife truck rattled through the iron gates and into the center of the yard. Two men in khakis climbed out of the truck. One looked at Brynna's attire in amazement, then gave her a sort of salute.

"Time for us to turn it over to the experts," Brynna said. Then she lifted her white lace skirts and marched toward the house.

Although Sam wanted to stay and watch, she knew Brynna was right. With fewer distractions, the cougar's capture would go more smoothly and he'd be up in the Ruby Mountains even sooner.

As she and Brynna reached the Kenworthys' door, two black limousines rolled into the yard and swerved around the Division of Wildlife truck.

Sam heard Jen giggling inside the house and then she heard Linc Slocum moan. She couldn't tell what Linc said, exactly, but his son's words were crystal clear.

"Oh, Father, give it up!" Ryan snapped. Then he walked back to the mansion and left Linc to deal with the investors, alone.

Sam was ready to go home long before they hung the two gowns and finished off the snacks. She ached all over, and she was anxious to get to bed early. Tomorrow, after all, was Monday.

Just the same, when they pulled into the ranch yard, she was glad to see Jake's old blue truck parked near the bunkhouse.

Jake wore a bulky denim jacket, but no Stetson. He kept his hands buried in his pockets as he stood in front of the bunkhouse talking to Dallas.

As Sam pulled her aching body out of Gram's car, he turned to watch.

"Go see what he wants," Gram said with a shooing motion. "I'll get dinner started. And don't worry about your chores. Wyatt's given you the day off."

Sam sighed with relief, then straightened her shoulders. She did her best to walk without limping and must have done an all right job, because Jake didn't get fussy like he had yesterday.

He gave a nod to Dallas, then strode toward Sam.

"Got something I want to show you," he said, turning toward the barn.

"I don't think I can ride," Sam said. In fact, Sam *knew* she couldn't, but she wouldn't admit it.

"Don't expect you to," Jake answered.

Sam glanced at Jake's face as she walked beside him. With his long hair tied back, gleaming and black, and the sun glinting on his dark brown cheekbones, he looked familiar and dependable.

She was sure Jake knew the truth, that she'd fall down whimpering if she even tried to throw her leg over a horse's back, but he didn't hint at her weakness.

But if he teased her, she was ready to respond. Once, Jake had told her he remembered Ryan Slocum as a jerk. She *could* tell him Ryan was back, and that he'd helped save the cougar. She *could*, but right now Jake was being a decent friend.

She'd let someone else tell him Ryan was back.

"Where are we going?" Sam asked as they passed through the old pasture and started up a path. It was nearly twilight. Gram would get cranky if she stayed out too long.

"Just to the top of the ridge," Jake said. He slowed his pace a little, but didn't ask if she could make it.

Sam heard hooves and nickering before Jake held a finger to his lips. He continued on silent feet, but Sam could hear her own breathing. Then she tripped on a root, yelped, and would have fallen if he hadn't caught her.

Two dark shadows passed through the gorge down below, manes and tails streaming as they ran.

"Who was it?" Sam asked.

"Moon and some mare," Jake said.

"Moon? He's got a herd?"

"I wouldn't call it a herd," Jake said. "More like, he stole himself some company."

"From who?" Sam grabbed Jake's jacket and gave him a shake. When he leaned forward, curling his arms across his chest and pretending she'd hurt him, she insisted, "Whose mare?"

"Can't say for sure. Both the Phantom and Yellowtail were chasing him down by Three Ponies. Then Moon herded her across La Charla and the other stallions stopped."

A vision of the Phantom filled her mind. This time last year, she'd thought her colt was lost forever.

Sam wondered what the next year would bring, then shook her head and looked back down in the gorge. Moon and his mare had galloped out of sight.

"He knew he was safe on this side of La Charla," Sam said. She rubbed her hands together, but she didn't need the warmth.

She was so happy Moon had found a family that she almost missed the small sound from inside Jake's jacket.

"Jake?" she asked. "What was that?"

He shrugged. Then, looking embarrassed, Jake unbuttoned his jacket with one hand.

"Since your mustangs are gonna be out of touch for the winter, I brought you a house pet."

Jake's big hand withdrew a brown-striped kitten from the sheepskin lining of his jacket. Awakened from its nap, the kitten blinked up at Sam and uttered a tiny mew.

"We've been calling him Cougar," Jake said.

"Jake! You are the best!" Sam squeezed Jake's neck in a clumsy hug. It hurt her, and it probably hurt Jake, but she couldn't resist.

"Careful. You're squishing him," Jake said.

"I love him!" Sam released her grip on Jake's neck and held the kitten next to her chest.

"It's no big deal," Jake said, but the grin on his face said otherwise.

Sam led the way back toward the ranch house, and when the winter wind brought her the sounds of galloping hooves, she felt cozy and contented. She and Moon were both back where they belonged.

From
Phantom Stallion
⚘ 7 ⚘
DESERT DANCER

It only took Sam half an hour to find two mares from the Phantom's herd. Ace's body vibrated with a low nicker as he caught their scent.

Sam drew rein, making Ace stay back as she searched the brush for wild horses. A flash of red caught her eye, but it wasn't the the tiger dun mare who always led the Phantom's band. As her eyes separated the mustangs from the terrain, she recognized two blood bays who always ran and grazed together.

The pair glanced up. Their eyes rolled, showing white around the dark irises. They were only jumpy, not panicked. Because Sam approached without shouting or swinging a rope, the mustangs bumped shoulders and dismissed her as a threat. Then they went back to lipping the sparse winter grass.

This didn't make sense. There had to be better forage elsewhere. And where was the rest of the band? Wild horses depended on their herd for safety.

"What are you guys doing out here alone?" Sam asked.

Although they'd accepted her before, Sam's voice spooked the mares. Hooves crunched on rocky soil as they broke into a trot, glancing back at her. One mare started toward the highway, head high, mane blowing. Then she changed her mind and both bolted toward War Drum Flats.

Ace gathered himself to gallop, but Sam kept him at a lope. Given a little space, the mares might line out toward the rest of the herd.

They did. The Phantom's mares were scattered all over War Drum Flats. Usually, they stuck together, in case danger made quick escape necessary.

About a dozen mustangs moved aimlessly along the edge of the small lake on War Drum Flats. She'd bet this was the bunch she'd heard neighing. They were uncharacteristically noisy for a wild band, nickering and snorting as they jostled each other.

What's going on? Sam wondered.

Mustangs were usually silent. Flicked ears might signal interest in an unfamiliar animal or tell a herdmate to look at something interesting. Tossed heads could mean irritation or a change in direction. The most violent battle between stallions could be triggered by a hoof pawing the dust. So why were these wild horses so vocal?

Sam glanced up the hill, squinting toward the stair-step mesas. The Phantom was up there somewhere, watching from his lookout.

Even without him, Sam knew his herd. Besides the two blood bay mares, she recognized buckskin, sorrel, and honey chestnut mares. That old bay was one she'd noticed before, too, but where was the lead mare?

As her eyes searched for the red dun with slant-ing stripes on her forelegs, Sam noticed most of the mustangs were wet and muddy. A gang of five young horses, leggy and full of themselves, splashed knee-deep in the lake, ignoring the calls of their nervous mothers.

A bay colt with a patch of white over one eye seemed to be the ringleader.

"He looks like a little pirate, doesn't he, Ace?" Sam asked the gelding.

Ace only stamped as the colt swooped after the other youngsters, churning the lake white.

Sam shaded her eyes against the winter sun and watched. They were having fun, but the frolicking colts and fillies were spring foals, the most vulnerable members of the herd. Sam understood their mothers' worry.

There were no biting insects this time of year, so the horses couldn't be rolling in mud to protect them-selves from bites. And the lake was as full as it ever got, so the mares and foals wouldn't have to wade out to drink. Why would the lead mare let them walk into the lake, where they were slowed by the mud and exposed to predators?

Shaggy with winter hair, the horses looked almost prehistoric. Beneath their wet coats, Sam could see their ribs. When Jake picked her up, she'd have to ask if that was normal for this time of year.

Jake. How long did she have before he showed up at River Bend? Sam glanced at her wrist. In her hurry to get dressed, she'd forgotten to strap on her watch, but she should have plenty of time.

Sam focused on each horse individually. At a rough count, there must be at least thirty animals, but the red dun had always been easy to spot. Although she was small and delicate, gliding over the desert like a doe, she had attitude.

The dun was always alert, always in the lead. Sam remembered how she'd backed down the hammer-head stallion who'd tried to steal the Phantom's mares. When the Phantom had been captured and his son Moon had appointed himself leader of the band, the red dun had kept her distance. Sam always had the feeling the dun allowed the young black stallion to practice being boss, though she was really in charge.

There was a squeal from the lake as the colt with the white eye patch bit one of his playmates. Sam looked the bunch over again. They were all babies. No more than six months old.

She was sure she'd spotted every single horse except the Phantom and his lead mare.

"Where are they, Ace?" Sam leaned low, pressing her cheek against her gelding's warm neck. If someone wanted to put the herd in even more turmoil, getting rid of the top-ranking horses would do it.

All at once, she felt Ace tighten. He flung his head

high and his nostrils quivered in a silent greeting. The Phantom was coming down from the mountain.

Moving with such grace that he seemed to float, the stallion left the ridge, following the switchback trails that crisscrossed the mountainside.

The red dun mare might be missing, but the herd could depend on their leader.

Sam sighed. Everything would be okay. It was time to get back to River Bend, so that she wouldn't have to hear Jake's nagging.

When the mares noticed the stallion, they surged toward him. Just as they did, a motorcycle passed on the highway and the herd panicked.

A dozen frantic neighs rose and the young horses in the lake responded by splashing toward shore.

"Oh no." Sam sucked in a breath. Caught between the mares and their young, she wasn't sure what to do. "Okay, Ace, it's up to you."

Sam loosened her reins. Ace didn't want to be caught between the two bunches of horses any more than she did. He sprinted along the lakeshore, running for home.

She glanced over her shoulder. The mares were racing after their colts, not about to let their babies get away. Most of the young horses ran ahead of Ace, tails streaming. A few ran beside him, matching his strides, mindless of their mothers' pursuit.

Breathless, Sam clung to Ace. She was surrounded by frightened horses. Her face was lashed by Ace's flying mane. She felt his strong, short legs thrust forward and pull back. Forward, back. Two colts swerved around a boulder, collided with Ace's shoulder, and kept galloping. They didn't know how to escape what had scared them. In fact, Sam knew they'd already forgotten the sound. The young horses were simply running scared.

For one nightmare instant, Sam thought of her accident from years ago. She could fall again. First she'd lose her grip on the reins. Next she'd bounce free of the saddle. Then she'd be tumbling in slow motion, hit the ground, and lose consciousness. But this time she wouldn't be struck by one hoof from one horse.

It had happened before. It could happen again.

Ace's choppy gait told Sam the gelding felt her fear. She needed to knock that off. The little gelding was doing his best for her. She had to return his effort.

Sam firmed her legs against Ace. She kept her hands quiet on the reins and settled her boots deeper into her stirrups. She would not fall. Ace had to know she was in control. Everything would be all right. She could keep her seat if she wasn't scared.

Ace settled into a steady run, letting all the wild-eyed colts but one stampede past.

Sam looked down on the soft bay coat alongside Ace. The patch-eyed colt didn't look like a little pirate now. He looked scared and weary.

Above the pounding hooves, Sam heard a mare call out. Then another. The mothers must have said something calming, because the young horses slowed.

All except for the little bay. He rammed into those ahead of him and stumbled.

Ace swerved left, trying not to step on the youngster. His turn brought him face-to-face with a second group of horses.

The mares boiled toward them, eyes wide.

A big honey-colored mare came right at them. Her breath huffed hot and steamy as her head swung right, then left. Her dark eyes looked confused. At the last minute, her knees lifted and Sam knew she was trying to jump the obstacle before her.

The obstacle was Ace. The mare would never clear a horse and rider. Sam imagined those heavy hooves leaping toward her face.

"No!" Sam shouted, but the mare was lifting off the ground.

If only she could fly, Sam thought.

But she couldn't. Instead of clearing Ace, the big mare slammed into him.

In a tangle of hot horseflesh and leather, Sam hit the desert floor.